THE DRAGON'S BOND

JADE DRAGON SHIFTER BROTHERS

MARIE JOHNSTON

LE PUBLISHING

Copyright © 2022 by Marie Johnston

Editing and proofing by My Brother's Editor

Proofing by Deaton Author Services

Cover Art by Get Covers

All rights reserved.

No part of this book may be reproduced in any form or by any electronic or mechanical means, including information storage and retrieval systems, without written permission from the author, except for the use of brief quotations in a book review.

The characters, places, and events in this story are fictional. Any similarities to real people, places, or events are coincidental and unintentional.

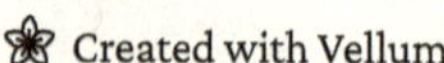 Created with Vellum

Lachlan

I was supposed to be a brutal and ruthless ruler of my dragon shifter clan, but I've defied the odds to become a calm male who thinks before he acts. I rule my small town fairly, without the bloodshed. The only time I acted with the same selfishness as my parents was when I selected my mate. And for the last four years, I've worried I ruined her life. I want to do better, but I don't know how, and if I don't figure it out, she'll be gone.

Indy

I know Lachlan didn't grow up like me. He didn't have a loving, supportive, and completely smothering family to dote on him. But when he announced he wanted me to be his, I was elated. I had high hopes. And then we just... existed together. A female dragon shifter is rarely short of pride, but if Lachlan doesn't talk to me, I can't picture a second chance for us. And when someone tries to kill me, I worry we won't be able to try.

L achlan

"HONEY, I'M HOME." I dropped my bag in my empty home and let out a weary breath. I didn't have to ask myself where Indy was. Out. That was all that mattered.

Away from me was all that seemed to matter to her.

After weeks in Garnet River, seeing my brother fall deeper in love, I disillusioned myself. I started thinking that since I was mated, my mate and I were in love too.

The love ran one way.

I toed my shoes off. An insinuating comment Indy only had to make once about tracking mud in the house like an animal had made the act an immediate habit. I'd never quit proving I wasn't the raging beast my parents had tried to raise.

Four years of being together and I hadn't worried about my footwear. It wasn't like she talked to me about her thoughts or opinions. But last fall, we moved to a new build. A nice house. One with square footage, acreage, and more than one bedroom. In case we had young.

Each year that passed, the idea of kids faded. Seemed like another false assumption I had made.

I unpacked my luggage and sent Indy a message that I was home.

A ding sounded from the guest bedroom next door.

Was she home?

The door was closed. I tapped on it. Nothing. I inched it open. The room was empty. The bed was made with the watercolor bedspread that had made pleasure emanate from my mate when she'd looked at it. A white base with shades of the sunset curling through it reminded me of the sunset on Mirror Lake. I didn't know what it made Indy think of, and she'd likely never tell me.

I leaned a shoulder against the door frame. Indy's honeysuckle scent was strong. Breathing out, I pinched the bridge of my nose. I thought I was building a house with extra bedrooms for kids. Instead, I gave Indy more space to ignore me. To sleep in a different bedroom.

The question I'd been asking myself a lot since I'd mated Indy and realized she wasn't thrilled about how I'd chosen her out of every single Jade female popped into my head. *What am I going to do about us?* I'd sworn not to be like my parents, but I came home every day to a female who'd been ordered to be mine. And I'd issued the order.

"Knock, knock." Levi Peridot wandered in. He'd gotten himself into some trouble with the Peridot clan. The only thing that saved his ass was that he was the youngest of the ruling family. The other thing that saved him was his friendship with the leader of Garnet clan, Brighton, my brother's mate.

I'd helped him some more and offered to mentor him. My attempt at paying it forward and creating goodwill between my clan in Jade Hills and Garnet River and Peridot Falls. He'd followed me back from Garnet River. I should've gone straight to my office, but I thought maybe, just maybe, Indy would like to see me after nothing but short messages while I was gone.

"Come in," I said. "We'll get going in a few minutes."

He let out a low whistle as he came to stand on the neat little welcome mat Indy put inside the front door. "Nice place. I was half afraid I'd walk in on a steamy reunion."

"Nah, she's out." I tried to keep my voice light but understanding dawned in Levi's gaze. Word traveled quickly in shifter communities, and I wasn't surprised people speculated on the health of my relationship with my mate. Dismayed. Ashamed. But not surprised.

"Sorry, man." For a young shifter in his midtwenties, he'd handled a touchy topic well. If he'd said anything else, I might've exposed the infamous Jade temper. But my tense relations with my mate had made the rounds, and he expressed empathy. Something I wasn't used to. Not in Jade Hills. No one dared speak to me about my personal life, and of all the things I tried to change since I'd taken over, I rather preferred that behavior.

"It is what it is." I sounded accepting, but part of me would never approve of the stalemate between Indy and me. I could do better. I just didn't know how. "How was the drive?"

"Quick. I was right behind you, and you weren't stopping. I finally had to take a piss at the border."

He would've arrived with me and witnessed my rejection. I almost thanked him for having to pee. I could've stopped ten times, but I'd had the urge to race home.

"I'll show you around town and get you settled," I said.

Levi followed me to my still cool pickup. "I'm sure I'd have no issues finding city hall, but I'll follow you again anyway."

I had planned my return for my sister Venus's and her mate Penn's departure. I was the ruler of Jade Hills, but with Ronan in Garnet now, it was best if one of my siblings was in town to monitor things. As my mate, Indy could too. She was a shifter and not a human, but she didn't show any more interest in my job than she did me. If it was possible, she cared less.

Once in the cab, I fired up the engine and hit the highway into town. I liked my privacy. My parents had put our life on display enough. I'd been an open book since they died in a house fire—to all of our relief—and I was tired of it.

Maybe it was because I was pushing forty. I'd like the last half of my life to be more peaceful than the first half. But perhaps I didn't deserve it. The sacrifice I had made stained my soul.

Trees with new spring buds crowded the narrow two-lane highway until a small field or pasture broke them up. Piles of snow leftover dotted the ditches. The far north in North Dakota got more snow than much of the state and stayed a few degrees colder.

I drove around the outskirts of Jade Hills until I reached a two-story flat concrete block building surrounded by a small parking lot and manicured trees. City hall, but most of us called it the old armory. It had once been a gathering place during the twentieth century when shifters went to war more frequently than they did now. The lower level was a gymnasium we had made into a rec center. It was popular with the younger crowd. The older crowd was reminded of horrible rulers and steered clear of city hall.

The place was only a few blocks from downtown, but some days, I felt like I was in a different zip code.

I parked by the door closest to my office. Levi got out and spun in a circle. "This reminds me of Minnesota."

"A little bit," I agreed. The woods were smaller but in a month, they'd be green and lush. Same with the pastures and fields.

Jade Hills was a small community. Only dragon shifters lived here. A couple of the bravest human mates as well. The surrounding communities were human, with wolf and mountain lion shifter packs scattered among them. Silver Lake, where the dragon shifter leaders of all shifters resided, was twenty miles away. The Emerald clan lived in a town not directly named after their clan.

Gemstone was planted in the east corner of the state, not far from Pembina. They were the most touristy of all of us, mainly so they could use the woods that surrounded us to shift and frolic in their dragon form.

Then there was Penopal. Opal clan. While our ancestors had been unabashedly naming our towns for our clans, those two had decided to blend all the way down to their nomenclature. Not a bad plan. I was just surprised my ancestors hadn't chosen Cower Before Jade for the town's name.

"The apartment in city hall should be ready for you to move in. It's on the second floor above the office. Most of the building is a gym. Only this corner has an actual second level." I had already explained to Levi he'd stay in the old apartment Indy and I had lived in before moving into the house. He'd be living in city hall. I didn't have state secrets he'd get into, not that I was worried. But I'd be a poor leader if I didn't think of it. "Otherwise, keep your head down. According to the council, you're here to help me adjust to Ronan being gone."

I wasn't lying to the council. They were used to my parents' reign and appreciated any information. I just didn't tell them I didn't need anyone to help with a transition. I hadn't even needed Ronan's help, but it'd been nice having him around. Levi needed an excuse not to be in Peridot Springs where too many people blamed him for a stalker following him into the woods and seeing him shift. The stalker had been a human, and revealing our kind was a major violation worthy of termination. His sister, Memphis, Peridot's ruler, had dealt with the problem.

"Appreciate it," he said. "What time do you want me in the office?"

"Take a couple of days off. Get settled."

He shot me a doubtful look as I pulled into town. "Think that's going to go over well? Is my clan's council going to hear about how lazy I'm being?"

Yeah, probably. Levi was a stranger and people liked to talk. Dammit. I didn't mind him in my business, but I needed a few days to adjust after being gone so long. A better idea came to mind.

"Go around to the other shifter communities. Introduce yourself. Tell them what you're doing here. Ask your sister if there's anything she needs you to talk to them about."

"Memphis will tell me to butt out."

"She might surprise you." I had talked for lengths of

time with his sister while we were in Garnet River together. We faced similar challenges as leaders with shady parents who'd upset relations with other clans. Memphis and I were trying to make things right. We'd seen the toll it took on our kind.

"You spent a lot of time together." His tone was cautious, his gaze guarded.

I frowned, not liking the censure in his voice. "*Talking.*"

"That's not what a lot of people thought."

"Fuck what they think." We were shifters. We could smell if two shifters were fucking. I had a coffee with Memphis. We didn't touch.

"I'm only saying it's how word gets around that might matter to you. I gave my sister the same warning."

Shit.

Shit.

If I'd had a better reputation before I married, I probably wouldn't have cause to be worried. But I'd fucked my way through the willing human and shifter populations as soon as I'd gotten my first boner right up until I was facing the *get mated or else* birthday.

Other shifters got a grace period after they turned thirty-five before they had to mate or get terminated. Not rulers. We were the example. Our aggression needed tempering, and growing old alone opened us up to trouble. A mate was a stabilizing force and another set of eyes. It was the way of dragon shifters.

I wasn't going to leave this mind-numbing job to my sister. She'd been through enough, and I'd done too much to protect her. So I'd announced Indy as my mate. Without asking her first.

And now she'd be hearing rumors of me fucking around.

"I've gotta go. Check out Silver Lake first. Deacon Silver stayed behind so his mate and his brother and his mate could go to Ronan's mating ceremony." I handed him the keys to get inside. He could figure out the rest.

I left him standing there as I jumped back into my pickup. Time to find out if my mate thought I was a cheating asshole.

~

INDY

THEY SAID *he's really into her. The way he looks at her.* One of my clients had brandished a photo of an intent Lachlan gazing at the sexiest female I'd ever seen. For a heartbeat, I thought, *Nice.*

I swiped my wrist against my forehead. It was cool out, but I'd been working in the yard all day. My parents had a lake cabin that my siblings and I were welcome to use any time, and I had taken it upon myself to get it clean and ready for each upcoming year. It just so happened to be the day Lachlan said he'd come home.

No coincidence.

Memphis Peridot was everything I wasn't. She didn't have to prove she was tough. She looked it. An edgy haircut. Dark hair swirled over the top of her head with shaved sides. She was easily six feet tall with broad shoulders and hips to die for.

I had smiled at my client as I finished her nails, told her *I'm certain they're talking about clan business* with confidence I didn't feel, and then told her I didn't have any openings when she wanted to schedule her next manicure. I'd be perpetually busy whenever she asked.

My mother jokingly called me the runt of the litter. Even before our kind made a pact with the powers that be to take human form and move among the up-and-coming dominant species of the planet, humans, we didn't birth litters.

I was the youngest of six. The tiniest. Mom was proud Jade's ruler had chosen me as his mate. *You'll have someone to look after you.*

For a species who prided themselves on strength, I was coddled for my diminutiveness.

I took my gardening gloves off and tossed them on the ground at my feet. After checking the time on my phone, I sighed and let my arm drop, my phone still in my hand. It was only four in the afternoon. If Lachlan had taken off this morning, he'd probably just returned. I chewed on my lower lip. Could I kill five more hours cleaning weeds and flower beds?

Scanning the property, I couldn't find enough to keep me occupied. I had cleaned out the daffodils and purple irises, changed the oil in the lawn mower, and picked up litter in and around the cabin, especially the ditch by the main road leading to the long driveway winding into the property. Whoever liked to throw their beer bottles out the window preferred Bud Light or Coors. If I ever caught them, I'd throw the trash through their windshield.

I had the garbage bag loaded into the back of my parents' pickup. My car was parked at their place on the edge of town. I could clean the inside of the cabin, but I hated to be stuck indoors on a beautiful day like today. The sun was out with big puffy clouds in the sky, and the temperature was low enough to keep me from being a sweaty mess. I might be perpetually frustrated and disappointed by my mate, but I didn't want to look like a disaster around him.

I wasn't comfortable enough with him for that.

The phone buzzed in my hand, and I nearly dropped it. Dragon shifter senses didn't extend into electronics. I expected another message from Lachlan. The last one said he was home and would show Levi around. So my mate had been home and discovered me out.

Did it bother him? Or was he missing his intent talks with Memphis?

I didn't know anything about Levi Peridot. Lachlan probably wouldn't tell me anything. He had assumed I wanted nothing to do with ruling a shifter colony, being so much weaker than him and all, so I had made a point to avoid all things leadership.

But several females in the colony had made comments, not just my client. Lachlan and Memphis weren't the only gossip. Levi's impending arrival left the clan tittering. Apparently Levi was a couple of years younger than me and as handsome as any other shifter born into a ruling family. But the message was from my mother, not Lachlan. **Are you still at the cabin?**

I was punching out my reply when the rumble of an engine caught my ear. Heat swept through my blood, and I rolled my eyes where it was safe that no one could see. I knew that motor.

Had Lachlan stopped at my parents' place to look for me?

He'd left me alone as much as I'd left him alone. The only time he wanted anything to do with me was when he wanted to fuck. And I was over it. I was determined to be more to my mate than a way to get off.

Unfortunately, getting off with Lachlan was unlike anything I would ever experience alone or with anyone else. The male had ruined me for others. Sex had kept me around for years, convinced me to stick around so we were more than a few verbal vows and a shared last name on paper.

The trowel, rake, and shovel lay by the flower beds. To give me something to do besides watching him drive up to the cabin, looking sexier than when he left because that was my mate—hot as sin and desired by all—I went to gather them.

Logically, I knew he wasn't desired by all, but he'd been with most of the eligible and willing females before he'd been forced to take a mate. And sometimes when I walked through town, I felt like there was a countdown on my head. Like some females were watching, waiting until he got bored enough with me he'd press for an open relationship.

One of my older sisters said I was putting my insecurities in other people's minds, but the dread had culminated to the moment I'd seen the picture of him with Memphis. I had my insecurities for a reason.

The engine was killed and the pickup door opened and shut. My back was still to him. I needed every second to steel myself against his flashing green eyes and his unkempt, dirty-blond hair.

"You weren't home when I got there." There was something under the accusation in his tone. Hurt? No, it couldn't be. He wasn't used to being rejected by females. He came from a family that didn't take no for an answer. His parents had taken what they wanted by force. They never used a tactic as subtle as manipulation. I had grown up under their rule. Lachlan wasn't like them, but he still didn't hear no very often. The legacy of his parents carried a lot of compliance.

I straightened, juggling the tools in my grip. "I didn't know I was supposed to wait."

He stepped close enough to take the shovel out of my hands. Consternation set my lips in a flat line. Did he think I wasn't capable of carrying a few gardening tools to the shed? "I've been gone a while. I thought maybe you'd want to talk."

I wanted to talk. All the time. Lachlan excelled in the bedroom. He could read my body like a billboard with an eight-foot font. But he sucked at communication. With me anyway. He saved that for his siblings.

Envy smoldered in my chest. I wasn't jealous of Venus or Ronan. I didn't think they would steal Lachlan away. If anything, they probably encouraged him to treat me decently. It was how freely he shared himself with them but shut down around me that I had a hard time getting over.

I strived for determined. Fierce. "I have things to do." To my ears, my reply sounded pouty.

His bright gaze scanned the property. Whenever my family met at the cabin, he went to the office and worked. I didn't know if he thought this place was a frivolous waste of time, but he hadn't said otherwise.

The crux of our issue. My insecurities bloomed when Lachlan said nothing to refute them.

I straightened and squared my shoulders, utilizing every inch of my five-foot-two stature. I was a strong, independent shifter female. I didn't need his approval.

That didn't stop me from wanting it.

"Have you been out here all day?" he asked.

I couldn't tell from his tone if his question was really, *Have you been out here all day and this is all you've done?* Or *Did you need all day to get this little bit done?* "I've been here for a few hours."

He lifted his chin, his most common form of acknowledgment. "Levi followed me home, so he knows where I live. I took him to town to get settled in our old place. He, uh, said that people might be talking. About me and his sister." The last part rushed out.

I narrowed my eyes. It wasn't like Lachlan to stumble over his thoughts and words. I didn't know if he strived to be the opposite of his parents in that way, or if careful deliberation of what he said was a recessive personality trait that hadn't been expressed in his mom and dad. Regardless, it was unusual for him to do, and he was doing it over another female.

"They're not just talking," I said flatly. "They're sharing pictures."

He frowned. A line creased his forehead as his naturally pouty lips pursed. "What pictures do they have to show?"

"I just so happen to have five images that were sent to me." My oldest sister, who lived in Gemstone, had sent me a screenshot with a concerned emoji. She had asked if I was doing all right.

My client had forwarded the one she'd shown me, and the last three came from females I had gone to school with that were a few years older than me. Females Lachlan had been with before. Unlike my sister, they weren't concerned for me. More likely, they wanted to expedite Lachlan going back on the market.

"Show me," he said.

The thrill surged through my belly. I could recite *I'm a strong independent female* a hundred times and it wouldn't stop my body's reaction to the command in his voice. It was the equivalent of a dog begging for a belly rub. I dug my phone out and pulled up the screenshots.

He snatched it from my hand, his frown still in place. I monitored his reaction as he scrolled through the images. I had expected him to be blasé about the rumors. He wasn't a male who wavered over his decisions. He issued an order, and he moved on. He acted, and he moved on. He wasn't a guy who waffled. But something about these images bothered him. Whether it was that they had been sent to me or that he hadn't been able to control how they leaked, I wasn't sure.

"All I'm doing is talking to her." He handed my phone back. "What are the rumors actually about?"

"She's a beautiful female. And single." Being mated wasn't exactly the monogamous chastity belt that outsiders might think. A kind that had a deadline for the single life found workarounds. They had agreements. I would never agree to Lachlan sleeping around on me.

"Okay?"

Did I have to spell it out? I pulled up the photo. "You're both turned into each other. From this angle, it looks like you're staring at her breasts." Memphis Peridot was well endowed and padded in all the areas I was flat. "And she's looking at you from under her lashes."

"I'm taller than her." He squinted at the image. "I wasn't staring at her tits. I was looking at the ground and listening."

He could've told me he was railing her, and I would've had an easier time accepting that. His blatant confusion was perplexing, and worse, it made me think he felt more for me than he did. "Whatever. You can be with whoever you want to be." I wanted to snatch the words out of the air. Hadn't I just thought I'd never agree to it?

But an open relationship was better than lying to myself.

He loomed over me. "Are you saying you don't care if I have sex with another female?"

"You're a shifter male." I made my tone as neutral as possible. "You're a ruler. You have needs."

"That's why I mated you."

Another chunk of my heart withered and died. Growing up, I had fallen into the same trap that most girls did. I had dreamed of who I'd be with, how madly in love we would be, and all the endearing murmurings he'd whisper in my ear. I ended up with the exact opposite. "Like I said, whatever. I'm not policing your behavior."

He didn't move closer to me, but somehow his presence intensified. "Are you saying you want an open relationship?"

No. A thousand times no. But I refused to be the helpless little mate waiting for scraps of affection that never came. "Is that what you want?"

"I would rip the fingers off any male who touched you."

I reared back. That thrill from earlier returned with a vengeance. I had heard every word he said, but what did it mean? "So you can be with others while I have to remain chaste?"

"No one's fucking touching—" His magnetism sucked away. Had it vanished altogether, or had he bottled it up and hidden it somewhere inside of him? "Is there someone else you want to be with?" he asked rigidly.

Why the change? For a moment, a spear of hope had

pierced my heart, casting light across my numbness. And now I could just as well be talking to a blank chunk of cardboard. "No one specific."

I let out a growl. This was frustrating. So damn disheartening. He never told me what he meant. I could only guess that was what he said. Yet wasn't I doing the same?

I pressed a finger against my temple. "Look, I'm not interested in being with anyone else. But this isn't working."

"What do you mean?" he asked softly. Again, he hadn't moved, the intensity from before diminished until it seemed like there was more space between us. It was like he'd been punched in the gut and the air had been sucked out of him at the same time. I immediately regretted what I had said, but I couldn't take it back. It was the truth.

"We're not a real couple."

"What's a real couple?"

"I'm serious, Lachlan."

His brows drew together and those lips of his that I thought about way too often formed a troubled line. "How would I know what a real couple looks or acts like?"

I blinked, unsure where this conversation went off the rails. Or were we diverging in two different directions with this topic? "Look around," I said cautiously.

"The only place I had to look most of my life was my parents, Indy. I don't know much, but I know they weren't in a healthy relationship."

Understanding dawned. He wasn't challenging me. Nor was he being facetious. He truly didn't know. "Venus and Penn. My parents. Healthy couples are everywhere, even in Jade Hills." Even after the reign of terror caused by his parents.

He stuffed a hand through his dirty-blond hair, silky locks my fingers itched to run through. "I work and I go home. And half the time when I go home, you're not there. Venus used to stop in, and now she's busy with Penn. And who knows how often I'll be able to see Ronan."

His tone was direct, like he was making a point, but a hint of his emotions was buried in his eyes. Those jade-green eyes couldn't hide the isolation he'd experienced his entire life.

Why hadn't I seen it before?

"Do you want an open relationship?" I asked.

He scowled and curled a lip up as if he was going to bare fangs. "Why are we back to that?"

"Answer the question." My words were a whip crack in the air between us.

He snapped his mouth shut, then finally answered. "No. Do you?"

Relief almost made me grin, but I put my energy into my reply. "No. But we need to work on us, from the ground up."

His direct stare bored into me. "How do I do that when I don't even know what's wrong?"

"By asking questions like that. Do you realize how little you talk to me?"

He didn't answer immediately. I had to give it to him, he was thinking about our conversation. He wasn't reactionary like his parents. I wouldn't have agreed to mate him otherwise. I would've run, sacrificed my life defying an order from the ruler. But while all the females were interested in Lachlan for his looks and the power of the position he held, his birthright, I had watched him. No hardship, thanks to his rugged good looks, but I had noticed things.

Lachlan was a contemplative male. Not the most popular trait in dragon shifters, but one that was getting more common, thanks to males like the Silver brothers ruling over all shifter kind.

"I talk to you," he said in a way that sounded more like a question.

"You probably said more to Memphis Peridot during your time in Garnet River than you've said to me in our four years together."

"We discussed clan politics."

I believed him. This male could be so frustrating. "Part of my point. You don't do that with me."

He frowned. I hadn't seen much discomfort run through his features in the time we'd been together. Lachlan Jade exuded confidence and a no-bullshit attitude. He'd been raised for this position and he took his role seriously. I was throwing him off everything he thought he knew.

And I wasn't going to quit until we either worked this out or gave up on each other.

TWO

L achlan

SHE SAID it was part of her point, but I didn't understand what the other part was. I could assume. She wanted me to talk to her more. What did two people talk about? My parents had discussed clan domination and how to get away with basically murder.

Clan politics? "You haven't shown interest in the clan beyond your family."

A choked sound left her. Dammit. I fucked up again. I was standing on a sheet of ice. It was breaking apart, and there was no land in sight for me to jump to. I was in foreign territory.

"You've assumed I'm not interested. I don't know what a mate's partner does. Your parents were also my only role models when it comes to rulers."

Well, shit. In less than ten minutes, I'd learned I knew nothing about my mate or how to treat her, and I didn't know what her pivotal role in my clan was supposed to be. "I don't know either," I finally admitted.

"Why did you pick me?" She propped her hands on her hips, the move pulling her gray T-shirt tight over her tits. Perfect handfuls. I had big hands, but her tits could fit into my palm. I'd feel the pebbled nipple against the palm of my hand and massage the rest of her creamy flesh with my fingers.

But I wasn't here to stare at her body. She'd asked why I'd chosen her. I didn't know the answer. She was eight years younger than me. Shy. She kept to herself. I was used to females throwing themselves at me. Some of them genuinely wanted to get to know me, wanted more than the status of mating a ruler. But they hadn't appealed to me like Indy's quiet nature.

"Did you know Venus thought you and I had already been together?"

Indy frowned. "Why?"

"I don't think she believed I'd truly pick a female I'd never touched before." I couldn't believe it either. But I'd wanted India.

"Did you tell her?"

How could I talk about the emptiness between us to people I loved? "You were a mystery I wanted to unravel," I said, hoping that was enough.

"Oh, Lachlan." Her exasperation was clear. What did I do wrong? She pinched the bridge of her nose. "It's just that... it's not enough for fifty or more years together. We need to know each other. We've been mated for years, and you don't know me. I don't know you. We need to start at the beginning." She chewed the inside of her cheek. Our beginning was when I announced to the clan I wanted her to be mine. "Take me on a date."

We hadn't dated. I'd seen her around town. She had kept to herself. Her large family was loud and boisterous, bigger than life, while she was subdued, almost demure.

Or so I had thought.

When I decided to announce she was the one I wanted, I had just seen her at the lake with Dallas Benson. He was her age. An entitled prick just like his mother, and the emotion that had wanted to claw out of my chest had startled me. Surprise had quickly morphed to rage. That male should not get to be the one to touch her. He shouldn't get to have her. To manipulate and use her like he had with his ex.

No one had been able to pin anything on Dallas, but the female he'd been dating hadn't been heard from since the day her parents had reported her missing. Then he'd set his sights on Indy.

A date. I hadn't dated. Before Indy, I fucked. After Indy... that was still all I did. There needed to be more between us. Mutual chemistry wasn't working.

"Where would you like to go?" I asked.

She furrowed her brow. "If you had asked me out back then instead of knocking on my parents' door and announcing that you had chosen me, where would you have taken me?"

"The back of my pickup." I owned a different truck now. Hadn't seemed right to be with my mate in the back seat or the cab like I had with the rest. "This is new to me."

"Okay. Um... you'll think of something."

"How will this work since we live together?"

"I'm going to stay in the guest room, and you're going to stay in the master bedroom, and we're not touching each other until we're ready."

I was ready. So fucking ready to strip her down and bury myself in her. But our connections of late had seemed more like sneak attacks. I'd ask some inane question, like what color she wanted the siding on the house, and then I'd close in. We'd have sex and then go our separate ways.

If maintaining my distance from her helped us, then I'd keep my hands to myself. "Okay. Tonight?"

"Tonight what?"

"A date."

"We can't rush this."

"A simple date. Nothing big. Like…" I racked my mind. What do people do on dates? Venus and Penn have gone out to eat, but Indy wanted to take it slow. Going to the restaurant outside of town would be too public. I didn't need anyone to witness how awkward I was around my mate. The same went for a movie. What could we do that was private in a nonsexual way? I glanced at the trees surrounding the cabin. "How about a hike?"

She scanned the woods. Was she thinking about her last hiking date with Dallas? I hated that seeing them all those years ago gave me the idea, but the devious bastard in me didn't mind overwriting the memory. "A hike? Nothing else?"

"I'll be honest, I'm going to be evaluating the land around us and whether I need to think about updates or extra security measures for the trails."

I expected frustration. A disgusted expression. But

she gave me an ironic smile. "Maybe you could tell me about it."

"You want to hear about that stuff?"

"Yes. I might have something to add."

I usually bounced ideas off my brother. Sometimes Venus chimed in, but she'd always traveled her own path, and she had her own business to run. Now that she mated Penn, she also had their new endeavor of improving online education for shifters stuck in small communities. When she returned to Jade Hills, she'd be busy. And I had no Ronan.

The low-grade anxiety that had taken root since I'd driven home from Garnet River upped a level. I'd never taken an antacid in my life, but I could use one now.

It couldn't hurt to tell Indy my thoughts. She'd been born and raised in Jade Hills. She was younger than me but remembered what life was like under my parents. "I could use someone to bounce ideas off."

Surprised, she drew back slightly. "I didn't expect you to like that idea."

"Go for a hike with me tomorrow. I might keep surprising you." I left it at that and pivoted to walk back to my pickup. I didn't give her time to respond. I had liked surprising her.

But as I got closer to my pickup, the burn in my gut ignited. Did I fuck up?

Dammit. I didn't question myself this much. But this was the second time I'd acted impulsively, and the first time had been regarding her. I glanced over my shoulder at her. She was staring at me, the same stunned look as earlier on her face.

Good? Bad?

She lifted her chin. "Seven o'clock. I told Venus I'd do

a couple mani-pedis for her and lock up. Then I want to hike to the border and see if the drones buzz us."

"I'll pick you up." A rush of humor flooded my brain. We still lived together.

Her eyes flared. "Lachlan Jade, did you just make a joke?"

The only time I joked was with my siblings. Until now.

~

Indy

I WAITED as Edna Seward finished admiring her new nails. I'd done a set of golden glittery gels that matched her horn-rimmed glasses. Edna was one of my favorite customers.

"You always do such a good job, dear." Her crinkled face creased deeper as she smiled. Her grin was beautiful and one of the reasons I had gotten licensed as a nail tech.

It was my due as the youngest. I had helped my sisters get ready for their dates—hair, nails, and spray tans. Then our parents had sent the three oldest to school. When the hoard ran low, the youngest three turned to cheaper careers to educate themselves and earn a living. As the very youngest, it was decided without asking me that I'd stick around Jade Hills and take care of our parents. The rest had mated shifters in other clans.

"Thank you," I told Edna. "But I save my best work for you."

Her grin deepened. "You're such a sweetheart. When

are you going to kick out those babies with that handsome mate of yours?"

Edna was in her seventies. Her grandkids were her life, and she thought babies should be a part of everyone's life.

The familiar pang tugged at my heart. But it was weaker today. After the talk with Lachlan, hope nestled dangerously in my chest. Did I have a chance at a happy life with my mate?

"Nature will take its course." Until then, I rigidly tracked my cycle and stayed far away from my mate when I was fertile. So far, it had worked. I hadn't been brave enough to ask him to wear condoms and admit that we had a messed-up dynamic that we shouldn't bring children into.

She beamed. "The practice is always fun."

I chuckled. Some might think she was rude or intrusive, but Edna didn't care. Everyone else got a nonresponse from me, including my family. But I bantered with Edna.

The bell on the front of the door tinkled. The scent of woodsy aftershave hit my nose, tickling it until I fought off a sneeze. My ex-boyfriend. Dallas Benson. In one of my more cringe moments, I'd dated him before Lachlan had chosen me.

I'd lost my virginity to Dallas. We'd continued seeing each other, mostly because I was bored and thought there should be more to life than taking care of my parents and their yards. Then Lachlan happened.

And Dallas hadn't taken the news of Lachlan's proclamation well. I'd been relieved to have a reason to break up with Dallas.

"Hello, Dallas." Edna's voice lost some of its shine. "How's your dear mother doing?"

His resplendent grin could make panties drop all over the county, but it didn't make one stitch quiver on mine. Dallas had been doting, almost smothering. He'd been a considerate lover, but he'd been so... careful. I had wanted a partner, not someone who thought I needed my hand held.

I wanted someone who created a maelstrom of butterflies in my belly instead of a male who left me feeling... slightly nauseous. Once with Dallas had been all I could tolerate, and I couldn't explain why. Maybe chemistry was just that important.

Lachlan was less restrained. In the bedroom—or on the kitchen table, in the bathroom, or his pickup—he dominated. Sex was the only part of our relationship he didn't hold back with, and that had been enough in the beginning.

"Mama's well. Ornery as ever." He gave Edna a wink.

Edna's smile was polite. She'd told me once that she'd been worried for me when we'd dated. Several shifters in the clan believe Dallas killed his ex. But it was hard for a shifter to commit murder and get away with it. I didn't think Dallas had it in him.

He turned to me, his eyes warming. "I know you're about to close, but Mama sent me for her favorite shampoo." His blue gaze flickered to Edna. "But I don't mean to butt in line."

Edna reclined in her chair and folded her newly manicured hands in front of her belly. "Indy and I weren't finished. Go ahead and grab the shampoo. I'll wait."

Annoyance flickered in his gaze, but it was extinguished as soon as I saw it. The first time he'd tried to smoothly placate me, I'd lost interest. And then Lachlan happened.

"I wanted a word with Indy," he replied evenly, smile in place. "If you don't mind."

Tension traveled on his words. He didn't like Edna's attempted interference.

I jumped in. My loyalty was to Edna, but this shop was Venus's. Mama Benson could deliver a verbal lashing that left a sting. I'd been getting glares from her since I mated Lachlan, but I could avoid her. Venus didn't need shit from her because of me. "I can ring you up, Edna."

Grumbling under her breath, she shuffled to the counter and handed me her card. "I was worried I'd hold you up." She raised her voice a few levels. "Since you have a hot date with that male of yours and all."

I almost groaned. I had confided in Edna that Lachlan and I had plans for tonight. Unwilling to make it seem like he and I needed work in front of the clan, but also excited to see how tonight went, I couldn't keep the news to myself. "I appreciate it."

Edna snorted. "He'll appreciate it more." She winked. As I handed back her card, she clasped my wrist. Her skin was soft from the hand and wrist massage I'd given her, but her grip was unexpectedly strong. "I'll wait out in my car. In case you forget to mention something about the aftercare of this beautiful manicure."

Touched she worried about me, a tad irritated she didn't think I could handle myself, but mostly wanting to avoid an uncomfortable environment, I said, "If I think of something, I'll let you know."

Dallas pasted his grin in place, and half-bowed when Edna passed him to leave. Tension radiated over his shoulders and his blue eyes were a shade darker than normal.

When the door shut behind Edna, I grabbed the bottle of shampoo he'd come for. "Your mom likes the tea tree stuff, right?"

"Sure." He slid up to the counter and leaned across it.

When I turned, he was there, practically hanging over my side. Thankfully, Venus had updated her pay system to an iPad. I lifted it from the desk and stood back to ring up the order. That put an extra six inches between him and me.

Invading my space. He'd been clingy, but in a way that made me feel like the needy one. I was the youngest of six. I should've been used to a lot of people around me, but not like Dallas and his calls and his messages and the way he overrode my ideas for his.

Lachlan was on the opposite end of the spectrum, but after tonight, I hoped we could meet in the middle.

"You and Lachlan have plans tonight?" He kept his question casual, but his gaze was direct, almost hard.

"Yes. He's been gone for a while, and now he's back, so we planned something special." I'd been sensitive about how my relationship with Lachlan was judged by the public, but I hadn't gone out of my way to make it seem like something we weren't. In the moment, I wanted Dallas to think Lachlan and I were stronger than ever. In a way, we were.

"Something special." Concern touched his eyes. "Didn't you hear about..." He shook his head. "Sorry, it's none of my business."

No, it wasn't. But I could guess what we were talking about. Lachlan's discussions with Memphis. "I heard plenty about it. Doesn't mean the speculation was true."

"The pictures were pretty incriminating, Indy. I'm worried about you."

And there it was. How people talked to me. Like I couldn't handle myself. Like I couldn't think for myself. "Don't be. No one would've had an opinion about it if he had been photographed with Deacon. Or one of the other male rulers."

"Does he sit in a cozy diner with them?"

My irritation was about to break through the roof. Lachlan and Memphis had been photographed standing in the street and sitting and having a coffee. Yet with all those prying eyes, no one got an image of them entering any other building together.

"No," I said flatly. "He's often alone with them in an office. But with Memphis, he stayed in the public eye."

Dallas's gaze glittered. I couldn't identify the emotion before he straightened and aimed his smile in my direction. "Good thing you're confident in his fidelity." His tone said that no one else was.

"He's a good male." I was confident in that.

A dark cloud crowded his congenial expression. "It's good you think so."

I finished his purchase, but he didn't make a move to leave. "I miss talking to you. Maybe we could get coffee sometime. It should be okay with your mate."

His snide tone put my teeth on edge. "We'll have to see." I didn't know why I didn't come out and say no, but my intuition said to sound amenable while not accepting his invitation. "I'm helping my parents a lot and Lachlan's home."

Dallas's eyes crinkled at the corner. He looked like he was smiling, but his eyes weren't part of the expression.

"You're always taking care of everyone and never yourself."

He hit on the conflict in my life. People took care of me, but only because they doubted my ability, all while ignoring how I was helping their world rotate. Up until my last two siblings moved out of Jade Hills, I'd gone grocery shopping with them, answered the phone in the middle of the night when they hit a bump in their own relationships, and went to Gemstone and Penopal to help babysit my nieces and nephews. But they questioned my part-time work for Venus, how well I dealt with gossip about Lachlan, and when I cleaned the cabin after storms, I fielded messages telling me to be careful.

It was like being told they loved me as they held the pillow over my face while I was driving them to an appointment. "That's how it goes sometimes."

He read into my expression for a heartbeat before he stepped back. "Well, when you want a friendly face to talk to, hit me up. We can go to Lacey's for a chai."

"I'll keep that in mind." I loved the chai at Lacey's, but only in the winter. In the summer, she made the best lemonade. Her peach lemonade was my favorite.

"Please do." He walked out, leaving me in an abnormally silent salon.

Was he serious about just being friends? We hadn't been friends before he asked me out. He'd been hot and heavy with Lily, and then when she disappeared, he'd been a hermit, looking distraught when he emerged to run errands. A couple of years after, he'd started behaving like the old Dallas. Several shifters refused to talk to him, accused him of being responsible for Lily's disappearance. But he'd seen me, the runt of the Nelson family, and that had been enough.

The Dallas in here wasn't the guy I used to know. He was darker. He was hiding part of himself.

Had I been wrong about him?

I couldn't have dated a homicidal shifter and not known it. Right? If I was so wrong about Dallas, could I be wrong about Lachlan?

My intuition wasn't wavering about my mate. I glanced at the time and gasped. Shit. I had half the time to clean up and grab a bite to eat. I didn't want to be late for my first date with the guy I was bonded with.

CHAPTER

THREE

L achlan

I'D GOTTEN HOME EARLY. My first day back in the office for weeks showed me how much work I had to do, but it wouldn't take long to catch up, especially without Ronan sitting across from my desk telling me about his weekend renovations. The council wanted updates on everything, and I tried to comply out of mutual respect, but I'd leave them waiting this once.

Where was Indy?

I roamed our front yard. I had thought I'd capitalize on my joke last night and pick her up. But she wasn't home.

I heard her car before she turned down the drive, going faster than usual. She parked in the garage and left the door open. She popped her head out. "Sorry. I'll change and be right out."

The smell of cologne slapped me in the face. "Why do you smell like fucking Dallas Benson?" I growled before I could stop myself. My hard-won restraint evaporated around Indy.

She rolled her eyes. "He stopped in to buy his mom's shampoo right before close."

"Why can't his mom do it?"

"Maybe you can speculate with Edna. She refused to leave until he was gone. She sat in her car the whole time."

I liked Edna, but now I owed her. I didn't trust Dallas. "Was he sniffing around while I was gone?"

She shook her head. "I'm not starting a date talking about my ex unless you'd like to share stories about yours."

I hadn't had a one and only before I mated. "I don't have any exes." Just females I'd slept with more than once.

"A lot of your old partners would disagree," she muttered and disappeared into the garage. "Be right out."

I continued wearing a path in our freshly grown lawn until she reappeared wearing tight black leggings and a sheer loose shirt over a pink tank top. The shirt revealed her lean but toned arms.

She caught me eyeing her top. "I thought of doing long sleeves to keep the bugs off, but I have leggings for those. It's such a nice spring day."

Being a shifter didn't make us immune to ticks. But that hadn't been on my mind. "Did you have a chance to eat yet?"

Her mouth briefly flattened. "No. Dallas came in before close and Edna was my last customer, so I always take my time with her."

"Should we, uh, pack something to bring with?" I hadn't eaten either. I never got nervous, but my saliva turned to dust when I thought of making a sandwich.

Various sandwiches were what I'd lived on my entire adult life. Indy had cooked the first year of marriage, and it'd been amazing, but then she'd quit. And since she was my mate and not my servant, I wasn't going to order her to. I'd cook, but she didn't need my bland meals. I put as much thought into seasonings as I did on what pair of boots I wore each day. I only owned one pair.

"A picnic?"

I had thought of munching on a sandwich while we walked. The trails around our house were well traveled by animals like deer, elk, and moose. We wouldn't have to do a lot of stooping to keep from getting snagged. A picnic sounded better. "Yes."

I followed her back into the house. She grabbed the bread and the lunch meat from the fridge.

I took out enough bread for both of us. "What did Dallas want?"

She paused with the mayo bottle in her hand and frowned. "I don't know." She stared at the bread like she wasn't sure if she should say more.

My inner beast raised his head. Something was going on with my mate. "What is it, Indy?"

I wasn't sure she'd respond, but she lifted her gaze to mine. "Do you think he had something to do with Lily's disappearance?"

"Yes." And if I could prove it, I'd make him pay. It was my responsibility as ruler.

"Without a doubt?"

I swallowed my pride. It wanted to know why she was asking, but snarling that the golden boy she'd fallen for at one time was darker than shadows wouldn't help. She was talking, and I wanted our dialogue to stay open. "There's something wrong with him, Indy."

Her shoulders sagged. "I got that feeling today too."

I didn't reply. What did she mean?

"You know, when you made the announcement you chose me, I'd been planning to break up with him, but I didn't know how."

Cool, refreshing relief soaked my soul. This whole time, I thought she viewed him as the one who got away. The one who was taken away—by me. "You would've disappeared too."

She didn't scoff. She scrutinized me. "You really think so?"

I considered the answer for a moment. My initial reaction was to say *hell yes*. But this was Indy, and I wanted to give her a competent answer. "Maybe you wouldn't have disappeared. He might've made it look like an accident. Two missing ex-girlfriends is too suspicious, and he's too smart." Otherwise, Venus, my brother, and I would've been able to find Lily's body.

The sandwiches were forgotten. "He invited me to coffee. As a friend, but I felt like there was more." She set the mayo bottle down and flattened her hands on the countertop. "No one knows for sure how distanced you and I are. There's talk, but that's all. No one knows it's been the same inside these walls. So is he gambling that the rumors are true, or does he have some other motive? Like you said, he's smart."

All I could think of was Dallas was trying to get into her pants. But what if he had another motive? "I didn't think of that," I admitted.

A pleased expression dawned across her face, and

fuck me, I almost exploded with pride. I'd put that there. "Finish making your sandwich. We can talk more while we walk."

~

INDY

THE TRAIL WASN'T WIDE enough for both of us to walk side by side. There was a small lake close to the border we could sit and have a picnic at. Mirror Lake wasn't as large as Silver Lake, but it was a local favorite.

Lachlan's parents' old place wasn't far away. Next to that property was the cabin my parents owned. Then a couple more empty plots surrounded the shore. And Old Man Redford's overgrown acreage. He claimed we were polluting Mirror Lake with our picnics and our hikes, and our fishing. He'd been known to set traps on his land. We all had given him a wide berth until he'd passed away last year. His kids had finally put the lot for sale. Soon a house would stand where all the trees had begun to die because he'd been such a tyrant he'd scared off the wildlife.

I reached the clearing and shrugged out of my pack. I carried the sandwiches. Lachlan's pack held the heavier drink bottles. He'd taken it automatically, and I hadn't fought it. He was allowed to be chivalrous.

I spread out a blanket in the higher grass away from the muddy shore. I sat and Lachlan squatted next to me.

He surprised me by speaking without hesitating. "I was thinking I need to do a better job researching the land that comes up for sale around Jade Hills. The town is in a good place financially, and it wouldn't hurt to expand the territory of assets owned by Jade. With drone technology and easy enough surveillance equipment for the general public to use, I would feel better if we expanded our borders."

The area around Jade Hills flattened into gently rolling hills, dotted with pockets of trees. Farms were plentiful in the area, thanks to the rich black soil. Black gold. "Would you buy it for yourself?"

He shook his head, his gaze distant. That had been part of what he was thinking about. "I'd put some of the real estate agents in town on it. Have them peddle the news around town and see if any of our local clan members could purchase it. If not, I can use some of my hoard." He speared me with a direct stare. "Our hoard. I'd talk to you first."

My hoard was a meager gathering of jewels. Dragon shifters grew their fortune, purchased jewels, and then hoarded them for future generations to use. Six kids were a lot of ways to split a normal shifter family fortune. Mom and Dad had encouraged my siblings to get a good education or learn a trade so they could build their own hoard. And there'd been me.

No wonder they'd worried until I mated Lachlan. I had a part-time job that paid a pittance, and the rest of my time I spent with them until they'd all left town.

I unwrapped a sandwich for each of us. He finally sat on the edge of the blanket, popping one knee up while he ate. He constantly scanned the woods.

I tried to be aware of my surroundings, but I wasn't on alert each second of the day like he was. His reaction was a product of his upbringing, and it served him well in his position.

I tried for conversation. He wasn't the only one who

needed to put in effort. "I thought more people would be out on a nice night like tonight."

"A lot of the clan is traveling now that the worst of the snow has melted."

I took a bite of my sandwich and chewed as I thought. "It was a hard winter."

"Yeah, it was." The gravity in his voice weighed on more than the topic of winter.

"It was definitely our hardest season." We'd moved into the house in the fall. More square footage. More space to avoid my mate. I'd spent the days it wasn't blustering and windy roaming through our yard and the trees on the property Lachlan had purchased. He hadn't discussed the house or land purchase with me. And it was hard to be upset once I laid eyes on the place.

I used to love being at the cabin. It was my oasis away from everyone. My siblings only used the place for weekend vacations that had become less and less over the years. Growing up, the cabin had been a guaranteed private spot. Time to contemplate my present and future.

When had it become an obligation?

I had a nice house with all the room I could want. It wasn't until Lachlan had left for Garnet River that I could relax and enjoy the beauty and comfort of the house my mate had built.

"It'll be the last hard season," he said. "We'll make sure of it."

My smile was almost shy. His confidence had always intrigued me, but I was dangerously close to depending on it.

A snarl rent through the air. I dropped my sandwich and jumped to my feet. Lachlan was up before me.

"Stay behind me," he ordered.

"I can fight."

The sound had come from the area in the woods Lachlan was facing. I had heard mountain lions cry and yell over the years. A few wolves that ventured this far south, and sometimes wolf shifters. The sound we had heard had definitely come from a big cat, but it usually wasn't so hard to tell if the creature was a shifter or not.

"Feral?" I asked.

"I couldn't tell. But something was wrong with it."

Another scream tore through the otherwise quiet evening. This time coming from my left, deep in the trees off the lake.

"There's at least two," I said.

He was a wall of muscle at my back, tense and ready to spring. Neither of us made a move to run. Beside the shore would be the best place to stand our ground. Fighting in our dragon form among the tight-knit trees opened us up to injury.

"Strip down," he said, his voice commanding.

Ordinarily, a tremble would've run through my body. But he was ordering me to undress so we could shift and fight if need be.

I toed out of my shoes, tossed my shirt and bra on top of them, and stepped out of my leggings. Lachlan was already naked before I was done.

The woods fell quiet. Birds quit chirping. Insects went silent. Our exemplary shifter hearing didn't detect movement in the woods around us.

We could shift and take flight to search from above where the big cats were, but it was the middle of spring, and the days were getting longer. The sun was sinking lower, but its rays kept the sky bright.

A band tightened around my lungs. I was already

impatient standing, waiting, in this position for something, anything, to happen.

"What do we do?" I whispered, growing frustrated with our standoff against an unknown source. It could be two shifters having issues with each other. It could have nothing to do with a feral mountain lion shifter.

"There's nothing we can do if they're not going to attack. I can't leave you here alone to go hunt for them."

I relaxed out of my fighting stance. "I'll be fine. I can shift."

"No." He shook his head, his gaze searching the trees around us. "Something's off about all of this. Get dressed."

"Lachlan—"

"Now," he barked.

I recoiled and spun around. He never talked to me like that. My mate was gloriously naked, but my furious gaze was on his face. "I can fight. Weren't we just talking about this? I can help."

Anger flashed through his expression, but when his gaze stroked down my body, another emotion took its place. Not lust. Desire? Yearning? "You can help me by getting dressed and packing up our bags. I'm telling you something's not right. This is an unusual occurrence that seems to be too much of a coincidence on the only night I decided to take a pleasurable hike."

Oh. He thought that whatever was out there expected both of us to either stand our ground, or they wanted him to leave me behind.

I scrambled back into my clothing. Lachlan prowled the shore of the lake as I packed our sandwich containers and the bottles of water into the backpacks. After I shook out the blanket and folded it, Lachlan got dressed.

Tonight was a waste of getting naked.

"We'll head back, but I want you in front. And stay close."

I hooked my backpack over my shoulders. "Do you think I'm a target?"

He brushed the backs of his fingers down my face. "I'm afraid that as soon as I chose you to be mine, you were a target."

I frowned and turned my face into his touch. I hadn't felt threatened during our time together. Other than females insinuating they could steal Lachlan's attention away from me, I'd been safe. Protected. "Promise to talk to me when we get back?"

He dipped his head, and I started down the path. With each step, my temper rose. Part of me welcomed the attack of whatever had disrupted our date night. I wanted them to pay for infringing on my time with Lachlan.

CHAPTER

FOUR

L achlan

Tension crawled up and down my spine as I followed Indy back to the house. We spilled out of the trees and into our big yard. Everything looked normal. A sparrow startled from the birdbath and the flower beds had been freshly cleaned. I'd walked by them, making sure there were no footprints or new scents around. I didn't trust coincidences.

On the way back, I had seen nothing and had only caught a faint scent of mountain lion. Not enough to determine if it was a shifter. I followed Indy into the house, keeping my senses attuned to the environment, and slammed the door, locking it behind me.

"Does Dallas have an affiliation with any neighboring shifter packs, like mountain lions?" I asked.

She carried her backpack into the kitchen and started

unloading the supplies we had packed for what was supposed to be a romantic picnic. "Maybe? He sells health insurance plans, so he's often on the road. Do you think he had something to do with tonight?"

Absolutely. "Did you tell anyone else what we were doing?"

She ran her fingers through her long, softly curling hair. "I told Edna. She mentioned it to Dallas. That's how he knew. I haven't talked to my parents since before you got home yesterday."

I wouldn't write off Edna as harmless, but she wasn't vindictive. She was a female who stood her ground, survived my parents, and had become one of my staunchest supporters. She'd been one of the few in the clan to openly approve of Indy as my mate. The rest questioned Indy's strength and submissive demeanor.

They had never witnessed Indy to be as ready to fight like she had been tonight. Brilliantly nude. I almost missed being able to see her dragon. When she shifted, she was small enough to tuck under my wings. But she was fast. With five older siblings, I didn't doubt she could fight dirty.

She was watching me, waiting for a response.

"Something's going on." I wished I had more for her. All I had was my gut and my history of living with shady parents.

"And you think they were trying to hurt one or both of us? You didn't want to leave me. Do you think they wanted to separate us and attack me?"

If Dallas was behind this, he'd want Indy to himself, and if he couldn't have her, no one else could. "Did you know Lily broke up with Dallas before she disappeared?"

"No, I thought they were happy together."

"He didn't tell you when you"—I hated saying the word; I hated picturing those two together—"dated."

"He said they hit a rough patch, and she wasn't talking to him, but he thought they could work through it."

"He was responsible. No one else had reason."

Indy folded her arms. "I'm not defending Dallas, and Lily seemed nice enough, but did you know her well enough to make a blanket statement? Even nice people piss others off. Or do you know more about Lily than you're telling me?"

Did I sense jealousy? "She was in the woods when Ronan and I were training. She had been running, almost frantic that she was being followed. Said that weird shit had been happening since she'd broken up with Dallas."

She didn't relax, but her tension wasn't directed at me. She ran her fingers through her hair again. "He's slick, but I didn't think he was a liar."

She wasn't defending him, but she wasn't as convinced as I was. Hate boiled inside me. Rich. The double standard that was fueling my rage. He got a part of her I'd never get. He got to have conversations with her she didn't have with me.

I started unloading our water bottles. I had to do something. Going out for a run and shifting was out of the question. I couldn't leave Indy alone. The sense that tonight was more about her than me wouldn't leave.

Fucking Dallas. If he was behind tonight, I'd fucking kill—

"Lachlan."

I snapped out of my head. Indy's amber eyes were on the metal water bottle crushed in my hands.

"Shit." I went to the sink to empty it, but the metal

was warped around the mouth of the bottle. I tossed the whole thing in the trash. Good thing it was mine.

"What were you thinking about?" she asked.

Did I tell her? It was humiliating, especially when comparing my dating history to hers. But I felt how I felt. "I detest Dallas."

"Yeah, if he had something to do with Lily's death—"

"Because he got to be with you. He was your first. You... talked to him. You two had a relationship." I hadn't even tried. I'd seen her, knew who she was, but I knew she was too good for me. Not that the others I'd been with weren't, but they hadn't wanted forever. They hadn't been interested in me. If Indy had turned out the same, it would've gutted me in a way the others' disinterest hadn't.

Besides, she'd avoided me as if she couldn't stand me.

She rested her hands on the edge of the counter. She thought for a few moments. If she was angry about my admission, she didn't show it. "I was sick of having no experience. Everyone stayed away from me. It was like they thought they'd have to take on my brothers to date me. So when Dallas was interested..." She shrugged.

"Look, I know I have no right to complain."

"No." She folded her arms again but this time her shoulders were hunched like she was hugging herself. "I've never talked to anyone about him. I told Edna we didn't work out and even when she pressed, I refused to tell her details." She inhaled and let the air out slowly. I waited, afraid to move or she'd change her mind about talking to me. "Being with him made me feel gross."

"What'd he do?" Being with Indy was heaven. She was more than a guy like me deserved.

"Nothing. I ignored my intuition and slept with him

anyway. God, I just wanted to do it with someone, and you were untouchable."

"How?" Had we been interested in each other only to avoid each other?

"You were too much." A blush stained her cheeks. "I couldn't have survived being shot down by you. Even though you didn't reject anyone," she muttered.

"Is that why you acted like I either didn't exist or that I disgusted you?"

"You didn't disgust me."

"All the females I fucked?"

She shook her head and hugged herself harder. "I cared, but you were a fantasy. If you did turn me down, I couldn't have tolerated being your only rejection. You were just like I said. A fantasy. Something I didn't think would happen, so it didn't matter who you were with."

"And then I picked you."

The corner of her mouth ticked up. "Secretly, I was elated."

She spoke in the past tense. Where had I fucked up? "And then?"

"And then you didn't give me any more than you gave anyone else."

I kept secrets from her. I hadn't known she was interested in helping me with the clan, but I had assumed she wouldn't be. That was on me. I couldn't tell her everything about myself. That was on me as well. How could I be open with her when she already looked through me as if I wasn't worth her time?

Tonight, the way she focused on me was different. But she came too close to seeing the real me. I was selfish to risk losing her. I'd figure out another way. "You're not the same as everyone else. You'll have to trust me on that."

Her expression stayed resolute. "That isn't enough, Lachlan. I can't trust you when I don't have any inkling about what you're thinking or the way you really feel. I need more. *We* need more." Just as I was trying to figure out how to overcome the latest obstacle, she said, "I'm guilty of this too. Telling you what I'm thinking is something I have to work on about myself."

Verbalizing the stream of consciousness running through my brain didn't come naturally, but my isolation had also limited my knowledge of her. Because I'd done that, she'd closed herself off. We were in a destructive circle.

If a discussion was what she needed, how could we overcome something as natural as our personalities? "Can't I just show you how I feel?"

She thought for a moment, her teeth worrying over her lower lip. "You mean sex?"

I nodded.

"I need more. You're my mate. I'm yours. Don't you feel like there's something missing?"

"No." But maybe...

Was that the restless feeling inside of me? I wanted more of Indy, but if she gave me all of herself, would I be satisfied? Didn't I want someone I could be fully honest with? I was closer to my brother and sister than I had ever been, but they still didn't know everything. I didn't think that would change how they viewed me, but I wasn't so sure about my mate. She had come into this relationship thinking she had bonded with a true leader. By birthright, I was. But how I came into my role was what left me feeling rudderless, unworthy to fully dock myself at anyone's emotional front door. So I concentrated on being the best leader Jade Hills had ever seen, just not the best mate.

She was watching me like she didn't believe my answer.

I no longer believed my answer either. "Maybe, but it has nothing to do with you."

She shook her head, rounding to my side of the island. Her honeysuckle scent curled around me. I wanted to drown myself in her. "That might be enough for any other couple. But you're you. Your position is going to make our life together harder. We both need to dedicate ourselves to this relationship. Each of us, every part of us."

I'd been able to tackle any project in front of me, even when the odds seemed insurmountable. But I didn't know how to fix this. I couldn't reveal my most shameful secret without risking everything that was important.

She cupped my face in both of her hands. "I'm not asking you to change overnight. I told you what I needed, and now it's time for you to decide whether you're willing to work on it. Because it won't matter how much I want us to work if you're not in it."

I opened my mouth to tell her I wasn't sure I could be what she wanted, but she rubbed her thumb over my lower lip. Lust clenched my gut and my muscles strained, insisting on picking her up and setting her on the island. I could tear her leggings off in less than three seconds and be buried inside of her in another two.

Her nostrils flared. She sensed my desire. I didn't bother to hide it. I was keeping enough from her.

"Think about it, Lachlan. No sudden decisions. We

entered into this relationship quickly, but we don't have to end it just as fast. Please, just think about it."

I wasn't ready to detour off my path of being a selfish bastard when it came to her. I bent to capture her red lips. She let me kiss her, slipping her hands around my shoulders until her body was flush with mine.

I wished this was enough. I could pour everything I had into a kiss, into sex, but showing her how my body reacted to hers wasn't enough. Still, I took whatever she was willing to give, invading her mouth with my tongue and loving the way she stroked hers against it. A growl left me, and I clamped my arms around her, pressing her even harder against my sudden raging erection.

Just as quickly as I had initiated the kiss, she pulled back. Her gaze stroked over my face and my eyes were riveted on her wet, kiss-swollen lips. She brushed her fingers through my hair. The tenderness in her eyes—for me—was humbling.

"I want to do more," she murmured. "But I want you to think about what we talked about first."

Now that I finally had a taste of her since I'd been back, I was committed to keeping her. I would think about what she said, and I'd also figure out how to do it without exposing everything in my past.

INDY

THREE DAYS HAD GONE by since the date night with my mate. I was in the salon, sweeping the floor when my phone buzzed. I went to the counter to peek at the message. The corner of my mouth ticked up.

Lachlan had been asking me out each day since our hike together. I was charmed he still wanted to be with me, and he was working hard to show me any way that he could without sex. But I didn't think he had really thought about what we talked about. Sometimes it felt like I didn't know him at all, but we'd still been mated for four years. I knew his expressions. I knew his body language. I had studied him long before we had gotten together. He was determined to make this work. He wasn't a male who gave up. I appreciated him. Yet as much as I wanted to give him my everything, I also wouldn't settle for anything less than the same in return.

His message was asking me to supper. My stomach rumbled. I had booked a full day of manis and pedis so I could work at my parents' cabin tomorrow. A storm a couple of nights ago had knocked over a few trees, and my brother had called asking me to take care of it before our parents tried to prove they were still virile shifters.

I'd asked him to think about what we'd talked about and he'd remained undaunted. I relented. I was hungry, for one, but I also wasn't giving up on him. I wasn't giving up on us. **Meet at Griffin's?**

He'd been back from Garnet River for less than a week and we'd had two significant conversations. More than we'd had the entire time we'd been together. If we could achieve that, then I wasn't giving up. Not yet.

I finished sweeping. The last task I had to do before I left was restock my supplies. Cleanup at the cabin might take longer than expected, and I had an afternoon full of appointments the day after tomorrow.

I usually didn't work at Venus's salon this much, but

while she was gone, I wanted to make sure her clients didn't take their business elsewhere. Previously, I had used it as a way to keep my distance from Lachlan. Long days like today, I regretted my choice, but it also helped. Kisses like we'd had the other night made it too easy to succumb to my mate's magnetism.

He wanted to show me how he felt. The problem was, I didn't believe him. How could I when he had put all of himself into the sex he'd had in the past? I didn't resent him for it. It was just the way he was. When Lachlan did something, he did it right. His pride wouldn't allow otherwise. He and I needed to be different on an emotional level, otherwise all he was showing me was that he enjoyed sex.

And since I enjoyed having sex with him, it was nothing but mutual fucking.

I went to the back room and loaded up with paper towels, cotton balls, bamboo sticks, and more cuticle cream. I turned around just as the scent of fresh rain hit me. I jumped, a gasp escaping. The cuticle cream tumbled out of my grip.

Lachlan snatched the bottle out of the air, but my entire armload had been disrupted. I juggled the cotton balls and the box of bamboo sticks.

Please, not the bamboo sticks. Those would spill onto the floor and scatter. I wouldn't be able to use any of them. I fumbled with the materials as Lachlan neatly snatched each item out of my grip until I was only hanging on to the paper towels.

I shot him a scowl, frustrated that I didn't have as good of reflexes as him, but more irritated I had reacted like a human woman being cornered in a dark alley.

He cradled the cotton balls, cuticle cream, and bamboo sticks and grinned.

I was struck speechless. Lachlan normally didn't smile. And I didn't mean that he only joked around with his siblings. I had seen him with Venus and Ronan too many times to not know that this male didn't grin. He didn't waste facial expressions on feelings that weren't inside of him. He loved his brother and sister, but he rarely talked about anything with them that would make him smile.

The grin was fading, and I panicked. I shoved the paper towels onto the shelf and put my thumb pad at each corner of his mouth. "No, don't stop."

And the smile was gone, confusion taking its place. "Don't stop what?"

"You never really smile." If he had, I repressed the memory. The expression wouldn't have been genuine. A grin would be nothing but a tool in his arsenal of being a ruler. If he can get his way without a superficial smile, then he'd do it.

His brow furrowed. "I smile." He thought for a moment. "Don't I?"

I brushed my hands over his face, ruffling the lock of hair curling over his forehead. I always had a hard time keeping my hands off him, but I managed. There'd been a shift. He was more inviting, and I was more willing to put my hands on him without having the move related to sex.

"I don't think you find anything funny enough to smile about." He'd had too crappy of an upbringing. I stroked my fingers through his hair again. "Too bad scaring the shit out of me until I frighten like a little human child is what does it."

The next rumble I heard was as foreign as his smile. He chuckled.

When he noticed my second stunned reaction, he sobered. "Are you going to tell me I don't laugh either?"

"If you have, I haven't witnessed it."

His lips formed the polite line I found almost adorable, a word I never thought I'd associate with Lachlan and his muscled limbs and broad shoulders. "I'm sure I have. I've had to."

"Not with me." Before the air between us could get too heavy, I added, "But I'm glad that's changing. Just no more cornering me in the back rooms of your sister's salon."

Heat flared in his eyes, and he crowded me against the shelves. If his arms were empty, he'd have caged me in. I fought the urge to take the items he was holding and put them back on the shelf so he could do just that.

The air charged around us, and he bent, capturing my lips. I didn't stop him. I wanted this and so much more. A small whimper came out of me as he licked his tongue along the seam of my mouth. I opened for him, and he lazily licked inside of my mouth. I stroked my tongue against his, so warm. I knew how good he was with that tongue on other places of my body.

A hard throb started at the apex of my thighs. I wanted what only this male could give. Being strong was the lowest priority for me right now.

But Lachlan didn't take the kiss any further. He concentrated on my mouth, on that one point of connection between us. I clenched my hands around the shelving unit behind me. If I ran my fingers through his hair or kneaded his broad shoulders, I worried I'd work my way down to his zipper until I freed that glorious cock of his and asked him to take me right here and right now.

He pulled back enough to say, "Fuck, Indy. You're delicious."

Dazed, I murmured, "That's the mints I was chewing all afternoon."

The corner of his mouth kicked up a hair. His full-fledged smiles were the rarest occurrence, but his almost smiles were as unusual, especially around me. This was a momentous day.

"I taste the mint, but you forget that I've tasted all of you." His eyes twinkled. "You're much sweeter than any candy."

I was nothing but a straw shack against the tidal wave of heat that hit me. A long, needy groan emanated from my chest. It'd be so easy to lift my long skirt and finish this.

Satisfaction darkened Lachlan's eyes. "Every time I peeled down those leggings you like to wear, I couldn't wait to get my tongue on that hot little button right between your thighs."

Oh, god, I was going to incinerate if he kept talking like that. But ruthless Lachlan was rearing his drop-dead gorgeous head.

"My favorite was licking you from top to bottom and feeling you squirm in my hands and against my face. And then when I put the tip of my tongue on your tender little clit, your whole body would jerk like I had touched you with a live wire."

"Lachlan," I whimpered.

He dropped his head farther, but not close enough to kiss me. "I think about being between your legs every second of the day, Indy. I think about the blinding ecstasy I feel when I'm buried so deep inside of you, I don't know where I end and you begin. I want to fuck you so bad I can barely see straight most of the day. I sat behind my desk this week so the town didn't see me walking around with a bulging erection. You mess me up, Indy."

I swallowed hard, my mouth suddenly dry. He wasn't a dirty talker in bed. He could scramble my brains and blow out my back without saying a word. But he wasn't a talker.

Had he been hiding those thoughts all this time?

Did it change things?

Yes. It made him even more irresistible. It made it harder for me to hold my limits in place and not cross the line to his side just so I could hear him talk dirty to me. But the last few moments had also shown me there was so much more to my mate than he'd let on. What we were doing was worth it. The distance we were maintaining so we could work on our relationship would be worth it.

None of that changed how ready I was to burn up like a balloon in the atmosphere. The curtain over a part of me that I rarely revealed to Lachlan peeled away.

I lifted my chin. "I think about it too." Emboldened by the way his eyes flared, I continued. "Last night, I couldn't get to sleep. I could feel you moving inside of me, the way you fill me and the way your big body covers mine. So I trailed my hand down my belly to between my thighs."

He towered over me, a burly cloud of turned-on dragon shifter. "And then?" he asked hoarsely.

If I kept going, I wouldn't get out of this supply room with my clothes on. "Then... I fell asleep."

A long, low rumble emanated from his chest. Despite

how heavy my breasts felt and the moisture gathering between my legs, I giggled.

Dark promise registered in his eyes, but the corner of his mouth crept up. "I didn't realize you were a cruel female."

"I was only telling you about last night. Be glad I didn't describe the night before." I couldn't bite back my smile.

He squeezed his eyes shut and groaned. "You would kill me if you did that."

He stepped toward the door. "I'm going to put these on the counter for you, but I'm going to need a few minutes before I'm decent enough to be seen in public."

Only the will of the dragon inside me kept my eyes from dropping to his groin. I had fallen asleep last night, but only because I'd been afraid a self-induced orgasm would wake him. If he had come to check on me, I wouldn't have been strong enough to turn him away.

"Lachlan," I said before he disappeared into the hallway.

He looked over his shoulder, lust still blazing in his eyes.

"Thank you." I grabbed a roll of paper towels and hugged them to my chest, feeling exposed.

He dipped his head and gave me one last long lingering stare before he went to the main area of the salon to deposit my supplies. I continued to hug the towels. He wasn't the only one who needed a few minutes to cool down.

CHAPTER

FIVE

L achlan

I WASN'T AN AFFECTIONATE MALE. I wanted to be. Holding hands sounded nice, but I never really took a female's hand in mine. There had been no need. But with Indy, I'd had the urge to twine my fingers through hers. I didn't even do that during sex.

As we walked down the block toward Griffin's, my fingers twitched. Should I?

I wasn't this indecisive guy. But everything with Indy was new. How I felt about her. How much I wanted her. And mostly, how I acted around her.

"It's humid." She squinted at the sky. Dark puffy clouds gathered on the horizon. "The storm is heading our way."

Shifters were sometimes more in tune with nature than humans, but we also had weather apps on our phones. "It's supposed to hit in a couple of hours. They're warning of high winds and hail."

"Again? I haven't cleaned up the debris from the cabin yet."

"Why don't any of your brothers and sisters come help?" I liked Indy's family. We didn't talk much, but they welcomed me. It wasn't their fault I got uncomfortable around large, boisterous families. Their laughter and the way they gave each other a hard time was like sitting next to a ticking bomb. Yet they'd never exploded. Inevitable or not, I sat there, not knowing what to do, and I hated being in that situation. While they were a decent shifter family, they tended to abuse Indy's soft side.

"They prefer to check up on me several times until I tell them I'm done and message so many helpful tips that I already know." She chuckled and shrugged. "I don't mind having something to do."

"Don't you like the salon?" The fact that Indy and Venus had gotten along eased my guilt over how we mated.

She shrugged. "I don't know. I enjoy doing these little jobs, but I feel like there's a bigger purpose out there for me."

And I hadn't shared any aspect of my job with her. For the last four years, she'd been like a fairy-tale character wandering the armory, wondering if there was a bigger world out there for her. And I had been the beast, keeping her trapped in my small little home. "You can do anything you want, Indy."

She flashed an appreciative smile, and it was like the sun ramped up ten times its usual brightness. "I love when you smile at me. I feel like the luckiest bastard in the world."

She stopped suddenly and turned toward me. I had the urge to shove my hands in my pockets and dig the toe of my boot into the cement. Had I said something wrong?

"I'm glad you told me. I'll make sure to do it more."

"I'll make sure I earn it more."

There it was again. The radiant expression aimed in my direction. Goddamn, she was gorgeous. She stepped close, rose on her tiptoes, and brushed a kiss on the corner of my mouth.

When she stepped back, she inspected me. "You look shocked."

"Is that the first time we kissed in public? Outside of our mating day?" I had given her a chaste kiss after we said our vows in front of the four city council members. After our ceremony, when I had finally gotten to be with her and learned she was better than anything I could have ever imagined, she started shutting down. But only because I had closed her out first. We hadn't bothered to put on an act the few times we were together in public. Our relationship wasn't the town's business.

"Yes, I believe it is." She tilted her head. "We'll have to change that."

"Looking forward to it." I nearly growled the words. Making that sound was starting to be common around her. I didn't care as long as she didn't.

I opened the door to Griffin's for her. She swept in, shooting a grateful smile at me.

A guy could get used to this.

If I hadn't gone to Garnet River to help Ronan, would we still have circled around each other without delving deeper into our relationship? I would never be so grateful for a trip.

My good mood veered as soon as I saw the hostess.

She was a female I had messed around with years before Indy. My mate might say she didn't care, but we'd test that. I could've waited.

Tonya's eyes lit when she saw me, and her smile didn't falter when her gaze landed on Indy. Tonya had mated years ago and had two young children. She'd probably gotten over me before her bed had grown cold. The best outcome for both of us.

"Lachlan, Indy. So glad to see you two together." She grabbed two menus. "Follow me."

Glad to see us together? I expected people to talk about us. I knew they did, but were the residents of Jade Hills worried? I strived to be a good leader for them. Being a happily mated male hadn't been a requirement. It was my own personal goal.

Tonya's greeting sounded almost... relieved. Were people rooting for us?

"How long have you worked here, Tonya?" Indy asked. I sensed no hostility from her. If she had paid as much attention to me as I had paid to her, she would know who I'd been with and who I hadn't. The latter list was a lot shorter. If it truly didn't bother her, then I was a luckier male than I thought.

Tonya led us past the wood-carved support beams and brown leather booths to a quiet corner. She set the menus on the table. "I started a couple months ago to get out of the house and have something to do. Corey's gone a lot during the day and on some weekends, so this gives me a chance to have some adult time. It digs into our time together just a little, but it's good for him to be alone with the kids too." Corey was one of the electricians in town. He had wired my house, and I had hired him because Tonya was a decent person.

"Oh, I agree. Mom went insane if she had no one else to talk to but all of us kids for too long. Dad seemed oblivious."

Tonya chuckled, and a sense of peace settled inside of me. Not because she was an ex who had moved on, but because the people in my town were happy.

"I won't be your server," Tonya said as she gestured to the booth. "But please, have a seat. And enjoy." She stepped back and hesitated. "It's really good to see you out together." Her gaze hooked on mine. "Really."

Disconcerted that the cover of the book of my relationship with Indy had been flipped open, I only nodded.

"Thank you," Indy said. "It's easy to let the day-to-day stuff overwhelm everything."

My mate swooped in to save our reputation with a spin on the truth that made us sound completely normal.

Indy quirked a dark brow at me from across the table. "Was that awkward for you?"

"A little," I answered honestly. "But it was Tonya, so that took the sting off."

Indy folded her arms on the table and leaned over them. "I almost died of jealousy when you were with her."

I frowned. Indy was cool now, but she hadn't always been. "You would've been a teenager."

She shook her head. "Didn't matter. I thought for sure you would see what a good mate she would be and you would settle down."

"Never crossed my mind." I didn't think it had crossed Tonya's either. I hadn't been mate material then. I was still working on that now.

"I like her." She dropped her voice to a whisper. "But I like hearing you say that too."

A laugh barked out of me, and Indy's eyes widened a heartbeat before she grinned.

Warmth spread through my chest, a different kind of heat than we had generated in the supply closet. The sensation was fuzzy, comforting, like a blanket fresh from the dryer being wrapped around my shoulders.

If there was more of this feeling in our future, I would move heaven and earth to make us work. As long as I could hide my one secret deep in the ground.

~

INDY

I SPEARED a sirloin tip from Lachlan's plate, something I would've never tried before. In our relationship, his stuff had been his, and I'd kept mine to myself, food included. If we shared meals, we sat in our spot and passed dishes back and forth to fill our plates.

He rotated his plate around so the steak was on my side, and he moved the plate closer to me.

Touched, I gave him a smile. "I just wanted to try one. Sorry I didn't ask first."

"You never have to ask. What's mine is yours."

I had to think about his statement for a moment. After our ceremony, I moved into the apartment he and Ronan had made in the old armory. Being the baby of such a large family and having never moved out of my parents' house, I hadn't had many belongings. Clothing, but no furniture. No dishware, no appliances. I'd moved into Lachlan's apartment, and it had never felt like my home.

Then he'd built the house. I had to give him credit. He'd tried talking to me about the plans. But by then, our communication had deteriorated to ineffective. He had asked questions about what I wanted for bedrooms, the size, and style, and I had given him the quickest, most basic answers.

Yet it hadn't mattered. When Lachlan was working, I had stopped at the construction site. I marveled over how beautiful the piece of land he bought was, and then my admiration changed to the structure being erected. A country home, cuter than I could've ever imagined. I wouldn't have changed a thing if I had been brave enough to tell him exactly what I wanted. He'd either learned how to read minds, or he'd had the same image in his head as me when he thought of what he wanted his home to look like.

"The house is beautiful." I had never told him. When he'd asked if I was satisfied, my answers had been short and succinct. *Fine. Good. It'll do.*

"You mean that?"

"I was impressed as soon as I saw the property. I knew from the blueprints it would be a great place, but when it was done... I fell in love with it. I thought you should know."

"I built it for you."

I was touched, but I wanted more from his reason. "I hope you built what you wanted too."

His expression shuttered. "It needed to be different than the house I grew up in. That was my only requirement."

He hadn't made many comments about his parents or what it had been like growing up. I was born and raised in Jade Hills. I was younger than him but old enough to remember the reign of terror before his parents had died in the house fire. "Well, the roof doesn't leak, and the siding isn't peeling, so that's a big difference." I held my breath, waiting for his reaction.

A satisfied gleam entered his eyes as if he'd been afraid I would dig deeper into his issues with his parents in the house he grew up in. "None of the windows are broken."

"I was never in the house you grew up in, but can I assume another difference is the lack of bloodstains on the carpet?"

He couldn't hide the grimness under the humor. "You'd be right. And that's definitely a bonus."

I pushed my peas around my plate. I had ordered the meatloaf, but the sirloin tip I had stolen from Lachlan's plate topped off my appetite. The juicy chunk crowding the edge of his dish tempted me to keep enough room for one more bite.

Griffin's had a few other families eating, but Tonya hadn't seated them nearby, giving us privacy. I appreciated her thoughtfulness. I wanted to keep talking to Lachlan, to keep getting to know the male I had lived with for four years. "What is Ronan going to do with his house?"

"He plans to put it up for sale and use the money for the renovations he and Brighton are working on in Garnet River."

"Are you going to be okay without him living in Jade Hills?"

Ronan had been gone for almost a year. Last summer, he had left to try to win Brighton Garnet's heart. None of us had been sure he'd succeed. It had taken them months to even go on a date. But I had noticed the change in Lachlan as soon as Ronan had left town.

He'd gotten quieter, more introspective, and he was an already contemplative guy. His sister was busy with her mate, and Lachlan had withdrawn more into himself each month that passed.

I'd been relieved when he told me he was visiting Garnet River, not so I could have some space to figure out what I wanted, if anything, in this relationship, but so that Lachlan could recover a part of himself. Without his siblings, he was nothing but his job.

And I was learning there was an interesting, compassionate male inside of him.

"And Levi? I haven't met him yet." I had heard stories about the Peridot siblings over the years. Levi was the closest in age to me. His older brother and sister were twins. Maverick was Memphis's second-in-command, her Ronan.

I had hoped Levi could drag Lachlan out of the shell he was closing himself in. But he'd left town almost as soon as he'd arrived.

"His first assignment was to travel to all the clans and make nice," Lachlan said. He took his fork, speared the last hunk of meat I'd been eyeing, and lifted the morsel to my lips.

His gaze was laser-focused on my lips as they closed around the tip of the fork. So I took my time. I released the fork with a tug, maintaining eye contact and moaning when I bit into the juicy meat.

"Fuck," Lachlan breathed.

I held in my giggle. Today was a revelation. I liked teasing my mate, and he enjoyed it just as much.

I swallowed and dabbed the napkin on my lips. "You don't want him hanging around?"

"I want him interacting with other clans without them thinking I had to make him do it."

I could see the sense of that. The other clan rulers were getting to know that Lachlan wanted what was best for Jade. Deacon Silver was a fair ruler, and the relationship between Jade and Silver had immensely improved since Venus and Penn had mated. If Levi made his rounds to the clans, they would either think he was there on his sister's behalf or that he was hunting for a mate, which wouldn't be a terrible thing for him to do. If he lingered in Jade before traveling, other clans would think he was visiting on Lachlan's behalf.

"When he's done with his visits, then what?"

Lachlan lifted a shoulder. "I'll find something for him to do. I think he's a guy who'll keep himself busy."

My mate liked people. A realization I should've made earlier. He spent most of his time with Venus and Ronan, and I had assumed he liked them, but I was wrong. He loved them. There was a lot going on inside of Lachlan that was almost impossible to see, and shame filled my heart that I hadn't bothered to look for so long.

"I'm sorry," I said, pushing my plate to the side.

Lachlan cocked his head. "For what?"

Tonya stopped by and refilled our waters. I smiled and thanked her, but Lachlan's focus remained on me.

"I've been upset for so many years. I felt underestimated and unappreciated because you didn't include me in your life. But I did the same to you."

Confusion continued to mar his features. "How so?"

"You like Levi. You're looking forward to his visit. Dare I say, you don't mind making him feel like he has a place and giving him a chance to learn new things about our kind?"

"It breaks up the monotony of the job. Is that all you're sorry for? For realizing that I don't mind taking someone under my wing?"

My mouth twitched. He didn't mean a dragon's wing, but I couldn't help myself. "I'm picturing your wing wrapped around him."

Lachlan's dragon was a sight to behold. The jade sheen over his scales and his impressive size gave me shivers each time I saw him, which wasn't nearly enough. Once, he'd crossed my path, but I'd been with Dallas and couldn't stare.

A humorous gleam entered his eyes. My mate had a sense of humor that I had witnessed several times since he'd returned from Garnet River. Yes, I had completely underestimated him.

"You're a whole person," I said. "I haven't thought of you like that. All I could see was the ruler who only talked to his siblings, and when he spoke to others, it was work related. I didn't know where I fit in, and I settled on thinking I didn't have a place anywhere in your life. I told myself that you must not think much of me, that you must've been disappointed."

"Never."

I gave him an appreciative smile but held up a hand so I could continue. "I know that now. You don't just like hanging out with your brother and sister, you love them. They're your family." It should be obvious, but the Jades were always viewed in a different light thanks to how their parents and other ancestors acted. "You have a sense of humor, a big heart, and you work so hard not just because it's your job and what you were born for, but because you care deeply—about the people, the land, and everything included."

He dropped his gaze to the middle of the table. He had one arm resting next to his plate, and he softly brushed his thumb pad over the tips of his fingers as he worked through how to respond.

Had I overstepped?

"If you're only just realizing that about me, what does the rest of the town think?" Concern was bright in his green eyes.

Sympathy propelled me to reach out and hook my hand in his. "They might not acknowledge every facet of your personality, but they see it. It doesn't register in words. It comes out as trust. The people in this town trust you, and that's not something you can find if you searched your family tree." His parents had been cruel. His grandparents. Poor leadership could probably be traced all the way back to when our ancestors agreed to shed their dragon forms permanently to walk as shifters.

Shifters have a long history of integrating into human society, the ultimate downfall of Jade's totalitarian rule. Thanks to the technology Penn Silver loves so much, Indy and her brothers had grown up with glimpses of a different world. They had seen happy families, and not only on TV. The townsfolk they lived among formed their own safe units and helped protect each other from their atrocious rulers. And Lachlan with his brain and compassion, Venus with her cunning intellect, and Ronan with his calm intelligence had all taken note, and they'd been determined to be different than their ancestors.

"I'm proud of you," I said, squeezing his hand. "You overcame a lot and became a really good male."

The gratitude I had expected to see in his gaze was

absent. Anguish took its place. "I'm not a good male," he whispered. "All of this is built on a lie."

I covered our entwined fingers with my other hand. "No, it isn't. We wouldn't be sitting in a quiet restaurant where one of your exes is making sure we have a private meal in a town where people keep their doors unlocked because they no longer feel like what's theirs will get indiscriminately ripped away. You've built a town based on trust."

"You don't know what I had to do." His voice was ragged, and I sensed there was more. The mate I had thought I was getting to know so well was keeping a secret from me, one that was tearing him apart inside. A piece of information that would forever be a wedge between us, the subject creating a cloud of determined despair around him that would not be shared.

Lachlan was a lot of things, but I'd always known he was a male to ensure the decisions he made were carried out to the letter. And he decided to keep a secret from me. I had an impulse to drop my hands away from his, but I ignored it. We were moving past that stage.

I squeezed his strong, warm hand between mine. "You can tell me anything. It doesn't have to be tonight. It doesn't have to be tomorrow, but you can talk to me. You will need to talk to me eventually."

He was still for a moment before leaning forward and brushing the fingers of the hand I wasn't holding over the back of my wrist. He opened his mouth and clamped it shut, his gaze going flinty as he glared past the empty booths behind us.

A cloud of woodsy cologne assaulted my nose. I had to release Lachlan's hand to grab a napkin to sneeze into.

"Dallas." My mate's voice was cold and unwelcoming.

"Lachlan," Dallas greeted with extra civility in his tone. "Indy. How nice to see the two of you out."

"That seems to be the common sentiment," I said, setting the napkin aside. I wanted to retrieve Lachlan's hand, but he'd folded them in front of himself, his steady, suspicious gaze on my ex. "Are you here on a date too?"

His gaze flickered, a dark storm brewing deep in his irises, and then it was gone. "No. I'm here to pick up some dinner for Mama. She loves Griffin's chicken parmesan."

"I've heard good things about it." I meant to exchange a look with Lachlan, but his gaze was zeroed in on Dallas.

Dallas adopted a congenial smile, aiming his grin toward my mate. "How was that hike? Indy was telling me about it."

I bristled, not from his words but the extra note in his voice I couldn't identify. The slick, oily feeling I had gotten when I dated Dallas returned.

"It was good," Lachlan replied evenly. "Do you get around Mirror Lake very often?"

The gleam in Dallas's eyes changed to a smug look. "It's a beautiful area. Half the town's probably hiked out there. You might get some visitors in your new house."

I straightened, my gaze shooting from my mate to my ex. Was that a veiled threat in Dallas's tone?

Had he killed Lily? Did I lose my virginity to a murderer?

CHAPTER

SIX

L achlan

I FOLLOWED Indy into the house, locking all the doors behind us. The air conditioning was pumping out cool air, and I made sure all the windows were closed. I didn't give a shit about energy loss. Dallas's words rang in my head.

You might get some visitors in your new house.

He had meant something with those words. A warning?

I could take Dallas. Whatever trouble he sent my way, I would smack it down like an annoying gnat. It was Indy I was worried about. Dallas was the type to exploit others' weaknesses when his pride was hurt.

I couldn't prove it, and that was my biggest problem. Indy might be able to take care of herself, but what if Dallas had already murdered once? Lily had probably been trained to fight too, like most dragon shifter children were.

I found Indy standing by the island in the kitchen, shoving both her hands through her long dark hair. The long pink floral skirt she wore brushed the top of her bare feet, and the loose white tank top dipped at her waist with her arms raised. She was so lovely, my chest ached looking at her, but she didn't need me stepping behind her and groping her tits or her ass. She was worried.

"He's up to something, isn't he?" she asked without turning around.

I hadn't made my approach stealthy, but I came up behind her and slid my hands around her waist. I dropped a kiss at the crook of her neck. "Most definitely. I think you need to be careful."

She twisted around in my grip, her eyes flashing ire and hurt. "You don't think I can take care of—"

I gently rested my thumb on her lips. "I would be worried about anyone close to me. And yes, I'm more worried about you. You grew up learning to fight from your siblings. I have no doubt you got a well-rounded education and a lot of experience. But training and surviving are two different things. You weren't fighting to kill your siblings. If Dallas is up to something, he's not planning to scare you. He's planning to steal you away from the world because he can't have you."

She studied me with her luminous brown eyes. "This is so surreal. In only a few days, I've gone from thinking of Dallas as an unfortunate experience in my past to a male who may have murdered a female who tried to break up with him and a guy who may be trying to hurt me. But we have no proof."

I touched my fingertip to the center of her chest. "You feel it."

"All I know is that I don't feel right around him. But to think that he's a killer? And that he's coming after me?" She shook her head, and I dropped my hand. "It doesn't make sense. You and I have been together for years. Why now?"

"It doesn't have to make sense to us. He could've been waiting for the right moment to strike. He could've been waiting for us to grow apart. He's smart. Hurting you would send me on a rampage. But if he could lure you away from me? Maybe that's what he was waiting for. Ronan's gone. I sent Levi to the other clans. He thought you and I weren't working, and he could swoop in. If I went after him, I'd be alone." He wouldn't stand a chance, but his opinion likely differed from mine.

"And Edna had told him about our date."

I nodded. We had no proof. Even if Lily's body turned up, we had no medical examiner to determine the cause of death. After shifters died, they took their human form. Nothing would seem amiss, but our kind was cautious. No outside authorities.

Yet my intuition refused to consider any other possibilities. The conviction that I was right would not leave. Dallas murdered Lily, and he was after Indy.

"I feel like we are working." She trailed her fingers down my cheek. "I had a good time tonight."

"Can I take you out again tomorrow?"

She smiled, feathering her fingers over my collarbone. "That would be our third date. Isn't there a certain milestone with the third date?"

"I don't know," I answered honestly. Her tone had

sounded playful, but I had no idea. Calling my past with women dating wasn't exactly accurate.

She laughed, a melodious sound that rocked me to my toes. I had never made her laugh. "I suppose you don't. There is a stereotype out there that date three is when one or both people expect sex."

"I'm not going to expect anything from you, or pressure you for something you're not ready for." I dropped my head and feathered my lips over hers. "But that won't stop me from hoping."

She closed her hand into a fist around my shirt. "We've already kissed. We can still do more without going all the way."

Hope surged as strong as the desire boiling through my blood. "Is that my only limit?"

Her pink tongue flicked out to lick her lower lip. I captured her lips, licking into her mouth to stroke along that tongue. A whimper left her and obliterated the rest of my restraint.

I lifted her to sit on top of the counter, then pulled back long enough to get her answer.

Dazed, she fluttered her eyelids and dropped her gaze from my face to where I was wedged between her knees. "Yes, that's your only limit."

"Thank fuck." I could work with that.

I planned to bury my head between her strong legs, but first, I had the strongest urge to kiss her. To just hold her. I always wanted my mate. If I could be buried inside of her twenty-four seven and still get my job done, I would. The urge to wrap her in my arms and keep her there wasn't new, but it was the first time I allowed myself to feel it. To hope that we had the type of relationship where we did stuff like cuddle and laugh together.

I'd made her laugh; cuddling was next. But first, I wanted to hear her scream my name. I wanted her voice to echo off the walls of our kitchen as I licked her to complete ecstasy.

I delved my tongue into her mouth and tasted our dinner still on her tongue. When she had taken my food off my plate, I had felt... I couldn't describe it. That warm fuzzy feeling crowded into my chest. She was comfortable enough to take my food without asking. We had cooked for each other before. An action that had meant nothing beyond sustenance. I ate my portion, and she'd had hers. Taking my food was a lot like flirting. She had never flirted with me until tonight.

I kissed my way down her neck as my erection pounded against my zipper like a battering ram. My cock would get ignored tonight, and that was just fine.

I slipped her tank top over her head, but left the lacy white bra cupping her perfect tits. I loved her boobs and the reddish-brown tips that peeked through the fabric like perfect little pebbles I could roll between my teeth.

Kissing each side, I worked the cups of her bra down until her nipples popped free. Then I took my time, licking and nipping until her body shuddered against me.

She gasped. "I think I could come from you doing that alone."

That wouldn't be new. She'd done it once and had stared at me like I was a magician who produced a tiger from a shoebox. Her cheeks had flamed red, and I hadn't tried since. As much as I liked making her orgasm any way possible, it was more important to me that she was comfortable with how I did it.

"Do you want me to keep going?" I asked gruffly.

She parted her puffy lips and took a couple of breaths

before she answered, her chest rising and falling, the saliva I left behind on her skin evaporating. Finally, she said, "I want your tongue somewhere else."

A low growl vibrated out of my chest. This female was fucking perfect.

I didn't bother taking her skirt off. I loved working it up, revealing her toned flesh. She wasn't a tall female, but somehow she fit perfectly. Her legs were long enough to hook her ankles around my waist when I was driving into her, and her hips cradled mine.

She planted her hands behind her and leaned back so I could work her underwear down until I dropped them on the floor. The material of the skirt had fallen to cover what I wanted to see the most.

A perfect cocktease. "Bend your knees and plant your heels on the edge of the counter. I want you fully open to me."

We didn't talk a lot when we had sex. I had been worried she wanted it over with, prepared to stop if she said the word. She had seemed to like the orgasms I gave her, but the distance between us when we were done had expanded every time we were together.

Tonight would be different.

She did as I asked, and that damn skirt pooled around her bottom, covering all the hot wet parts I wanted to get my mouth on.

I flipped the material up to her belly and let out a guttural groan.

"So fucking wet and ready." I met her gaze, floored by the touch of insecurity I saw in her eyes. I needed to change that. "Do you know how crazy you drive me, Indy?"

She shook her head. "How? Why?"

I had the same questions. How could she not see she drove me crazy? Why didn't she know? The answer was in my failure to communicate. I had been too afraid to give her a glimpse of my dark corners, and I had closed her off to everything.

I traced a finger through her wet seam. "You're beautiful, for one. I like the way you watch what's happening before you react. You're not volatile." I reversed the path I had taken with my finger, and her thighs quivered. "I see how you take care of your parents. You're dependable, and I don't know why that's not a complete turn-on for more people. You speak your mind, but you do it in a way that sneaks up on a person. They have no idea you were blunt with them because you're also considerate. That gets me rock fucking hard, Indy."

She licked her lips again, and I was tempted to capture her tongue once more. "Dependable and considerate. Not exactly the traits I thought would catch the most desired male in town."

"Everything about you is perfection. And after our first night together, I couldn't believe you were real."

She rolled her hips up. "God, Lachlan. It's a good thing you didn't talk like this from the beginning, or I would've been lost before I knew what I wanted out of us."

"You need to tell me." I couldn't forget how she was open to me or how my erection was angry it wasn't getting to touch her, but I focused on my words. Everything else fell away. "Tell me what you want out of me, out of us. I don't want to mess this up again."

"I will." She was breathless. "But I have to admit, I can't quite think right now. I want you so bad."

I wouldn't keep her waiting. I braced my arms under

her ass and pulled her to my face. And I devoured her. I attacked her clit like my job was to wring three orgasms from her in the next five minutes.

The first one hit almost immediately, her powerful climax exploding against my tongue. I kept going. It wasn't enough.

"Lachlan!" She writhed against me. Her ass bucked off the surface of the counter, but I caught her and held her still. Ruthlessly, I launched all of my knowledge. The pressure. The tiny strokes. She especially liked when I flattened my tongue against her. She came again, my name a long moan.

For her third orgasm, I pressed a finger inside of her. Her greedy body clamped around me and I squeezed a second finger inside, loving the way she immediately started riding my fingers.

"Lachlan," she gasped. "I don't think I can do this again."

"Do you want me to stop?" I breathed against her sensitive flesh.

"God, no."

Grinning, I concentrated on my task. Another explosion, longer and slower, I wrung the third orgasm out of her.

She collapsed on the surface of the counter, her arms sprawled above her head and her knees relaxed to the sides. She was completely open to me, trusting me to do anything I wanted with her body except step past the limit she had set.

As taut as my body was, as much as need pounded against every vessel in my dick, all I wanted to do was carry this wanton goddess to my bed. To our bed.

"I want to hold you." My voice came out coarse. I

should head straight to the shower and blast my crotch with ice water while I jacked off. But I could control myself as long as she was in my arms.

She rolled her head to the side, giving me a dreamy, satisfied look. "Take me to our bedroom, Lachlan."

~

INDY

I HAD DOZED off for a few hours, cocooned in my mate's embrace. We had never slept like this. A few times, I had woken up pressed into his side, but I had quickly extracted myself before my heart had become as involved as my body.

There would be no extraction tonight. My body hummed from what he had done earlier. Being with him was usually explosive, that was nothing new. But the evening had been... Phenomenal. There had been a connection between us. Lachlan hadn't made me feel used before, but I'd been left with the sense of what now. The question no longer plagued me. I meant something to him, and he was trying to show me. Soon, he would be able to tell me. The part of himself he was holding back would be mine.

I wouldn't settle for less.

Rolling to my other side, I pressed my face against his bare chest. He had undressed down to his boxer briefs as if the flimsy fabric were enough to hold back the giant erection he'd been sporting all night. He hadn't pressed for more.

His breathing was even, but he wasn't asleep. I

wanted to keep the night going. Before the early rays of dawn peeked through the window and reminded us of our obligations, I wanted more time in the quiet dark with him.

I trailed my fingers over his defined pecs, then moved down the ripples of his abs. He wasn't fastidious about his workout regimen or his diet, but he somehow kept the same spectacular shape through the years. The male was approaching his forties, and even as a dragon shifter, he had the body of someone fifteen years younger.

"You don't have to do that," he rumbled as my hand approached the waistband of his underwear.

"I want to." I lifted my head to meet his hooded but sharp gaze. "Do you want me to?" The consideration he had shown wasn't lost on me.

"More than anything." He wrapped his powerful hand around mine. "I just want to make sure you know what I did earlier wasn't based on some quid pro quo concept."

"I know. I know that about you." In one motion, I rolled to my knees and straddled his legs. Scooting down, I took his underwear with me. If he had softened at all after what he had done to me on the island, all the blood had returned. His proud erection jutted into the shadows of the night, as proud and powerfully built as the rest of him.

I had done this for him before. I'd gotten him off with my mouth and my hands. I might not have known what he thought about me or why he had chosen me, but I had known that I wanted to give as good as I got.

I didn't take him into my mouth right away. Stroking my hand up and down his hot length, I watched the way his abs clenched and listened to the low moan that vibrated his rib cage.

"I want this image of you in my head for the rest of my life." His voice was low, barely a whisper. He fisted the sheets with his hands but didn't interfere with my lazy pumps. "The way your dark hair is wild around your head, falling against your bronzed skin, and that look in your eye…"

"What?" I asked, breathless to hear how he saw me.

"The way your amber irises get darker when you're turned on." With shifter's enhanced senses, he'd be able to tell in the dark room. "The lingering uncertainty residing inside of you when we're usually together is gone. You've always been confident about yourself, but the way you are now? You have no question about us. I could get used to that."

He wanted to make sure he put that look in my eye permanently, but he spoke as if it was temporary.

"We're working on it, Lachlan. Just keep doing what you're doing, and we'll be fine."

And there was a flash of uncertainty. Of stubborn determination he knew was wrong, but insisted on traveling down the same path anyway. What wasn't he telling me?

It was early for us yet. We had only begun working on strengthening our bond. He would tell me in time. I had to be sure of it. We were working so well together, and last night had been as magical as this moment was promising to be.

I would lose myself in giving him pleasure. Just as I was trusting him, he needed to be able to trust me with his deepest and darkest secrets. We weren't just any couple in this clan; we were the ruling couple, and if we weren't strong, it threatened all of our people.

I bent over him, taking the searing hot tip of him between my lips and sucking him down as far as he could go. His salty flavor hit my tongue, and I let out a groan that traveled from my chest into his thighs where my breasts were brushing against his skin. The soft hair on his thighs tickled the tips of my nipples, sending an arc of electricity between us.

He went rigid, fisting the sheets so hard he pulled two of the ends free. I kept going. Bobbing my head up and down, I used all the tools in my arsenal. He liked when I swirled my tongue at the tip and flicked it across his broad head. He liked when I pumped the base of his cock and cradled his balls. He especially liked how I trapped him between my legs and that I was completely naked.

I liked how he gave so freely but held himself back. He could flip me sideways and bury himself inside and I wouldn't argue. With the way a steady throb had settled between my legs. I'd be putty in his hands.

But he pumped his hips only enough to keep from gagging me. His legs were tense like he wanted to press his heels into the mattress and ram his hips up just to get farther down my throat, but he didn't. I had a powerful male underneath me and in my mouth, and he held himself back so I could have my fun.

"Indy—" My name choked off as he slammed into his climax and exploded in my mouth. His roar echoed off the walls as I drank him down and carried him through the orgasm.

This moment of vulnerability, where he was all mine, where he allowed me to have control over what was happening, was intoxicating. If I was a bigger person, I wouldn't admit that this was what had kept me living in the same house as him. These moments I experienced with him had given me hope, had shown me I wanted more between us than some law dictating he had to be mated.

When he went still, I released him and crawled back up his body to tuck myself under his arm. He hugged me to his side, but didn't otherwise move the rest of his body. He was spent, his chest rapidly rising and falling.

A mating was forever, but that didn't stop unhappy couples from roaming outside their vows. It worked for several people I know in Jade Hills and other clans, but the arrangement was nothing I had wanted for myself.

This was what I had wanted. One male who was all mine.

"Thank you," he said, his eyes still closed.

I traced my fingers over the fevered skin of his chest. "There's nothing to thank me for. Tonight has been really special."

He gripped my hand gently in his and brought my fingers to his mouth. He brushed soft kisses over the backs and settled our linked hands on his chest. "I still want to take you out tomorrow night, but I don't expect you to sleep with me."

We shouldn't have sex yet. He was still holding back, and I was standing on his doorstep with my heart in my hands, ready to give him everything. "I want to be with you tomorrow night too. In every way possible. But I don't know if we've come far enough yet." I peeked at his chiseled face for his reaction.

Grim acceptance resonated in his features. What wasn't he telling me?

I thought about what we had just done and how

much progress we had made in such a short amount of time. "I know it seems silly. We're getting each other off, and we've had sex before. It's a flimsy limit that seems to have no meaning."

"It's symbolic. It means something."

"I wish you'd talk to me about what's bothering you."

He dropped his stare from the ceiling to meet my gaze. "If it makes you feel better, it is not something I've talked to anyone about. It's something I plan to take to the grave, for everyone's benefit."

Curiosity bubbled like a hot tar pit inside me. What could he be hiding that left him with shame and the fear that he would unravel if we learned what had happened?

I'd had a large family, and while I often felt lost in the chaos, I'd had my parents to talk to. My siblings. They had all moved away, but we messaged and chatted. I even had Venus and my clients to speak with.

Was the problem as simple, yet as complicated, as Lachlan's inexperience with a support system? Growing up, I was sure he had taken his role of protector for his siblings seriously. It was his identity. No matter how close he got with Venus and Ronan, his first priority would always be to watch over them. He would be the same with me.

We'd work on that. My superficial no-sex rule would be the ultimate symbol of our trust and confidence in each other. I was more than an obligation to him, I just had to show him.

SEVEN

L achlan

I'D BEEN at work for a little over an hour, and I'd done nothing but stare at the top of my desk. If another shifter walked into my office, they'd slam into a wall of my arousal.

Being with Indy had always been a step apart from my past experiences. She had meant more, and being with her had always filled an empty well inside of me that had been parched for most of my life.

But last night...

Damn.

After she had sucked me off and we had talked, I had planned to go back to sleep. She was working at the cabin all day and could have used the rest. Instead, I had spun her around and sixty-nined the ever-loving hell out of her until the sun had cleared the horizon.

I could drive over to the cabin and do the same to her for the rest of the day.

My need for her was growing stronger. My confession hovered on my tongue. But she couldn't know. A challenge to me would extend to her. As my mate, she was an extension of me.

A message from Ronan popped onto my phone screen, dragging my attention to the phone sitting on my desk. **How's it going?**

I frowned. Ronan and I didn't usually message just because. In recent years, we'd had to update each other on what was going on with Venus and the mating contract between her and Deacon. Then Deacon had met and fallen in love with Ava, and Ronan and I had switched our attention to Deacon's brother and his determined pursuit of our sister.

Then Ronan had gone to Garnet River, and I'd had to stay in contact to ensure he was making progress. Before all that was typical clan bullshit, preceded by mitigating the trauma our parents caused with their very existence.

I punched in the message back to him. **Fine. How was the ceremony?**

I'd hated missing his mating ceremony to Brighton, but Venus and Brighton were friends. It made more sense for my sister to be in Garnet River than me, and one of the Jade ruling family had to be in town.

And I had missed my mate. She could have been in charge of Jade Hills while I was gone, but I hadn't discussed my work with her. Maybe we could talk about this job and her role as my mate when we met for dinner tonight.

I didn't know what our plans were, and I didn't care as long as I got to be with her.

My phone rang. Ronan.

I answered. "Yeah?"

"The ceremony was like any other mating ceremony, only it was fucking awesome because it was mine," Ronan said. "And I missed half the reception because I dragged Brighton away to have sex."

"Sounds like a successful day."

Ronan chuckled. "I'm just calling to check in. I know I've been gone for almost a year, but it's weird I'm not going back." Ronan had left with the thought that he and Brighton would be good for each other, but he wasn't going to force it, and Deacon wouldn't order it as the Silver ruler over all shifters.

"It's going to take some getting used to. I sent Levi to go talk to the other ruling families."

"Unsupervised?"

"After what happened with that human that learned what he was, he has to prove to all the clans he's capable."

The incident wasn't necessarily Levi's fault. A human man who had been harassing Brighton tried following Levi to get to her. He'd trailed Levi to the woods and saw him shift. Then he had tried blackmailing Levi, but Memphis took care of the man. Termination was sometimes the only way to protect our kind's secrets.

But the responsibility rested on Levi's shoulders, and Peridot's city council had wanted him held accountable. Levi was part of a ruling family, and we were examples. Sometimes our punishments were more severe.

Peridot's council wanted Levi to settle down, and in their mind, that meant mating. Memphis and I had come up with another way to make it look like he was growing up and maturing when it was only an illusion. Levi

Peridot might be young, but he was a decent guy. Regardless, it was good for him to get out among the other clans. As isolated in Minnesota as Peridot was, it wasn't easy for him to find someone to be with.

"You gave him the shifter version of musical chairs, Tinder style."

Busted. If Levi found someone to settle down with, it solved his problem in a heartbeat. "Either way, it's going to help him. And if he has to settle in Jade Hills for a while... That's not the end of the world."

There was a beat of silence on the other end. "You really don't mind having him around?"

I didn't. The revelation surprised me as much as them. I didn't go out of my way to be alone, but my actions were interwoven into my lifestyle. It had been easy for Indy to distance herself from me. "It'll be good for both of us. This position is better when there's someone around to talk with."

"So nothing has changed otherwise?" Disappointment resounded in his voice.

It took me a moment to understand what he meant. "No, there have been some changes. Indy wasn't home when I arrived."

"That's nothing new." Ronan might have meant it as playful before, but this time, I detected compassion in his tone.

"Except when I found her, we talked." I stopped to organize what I wanted to say. Talking about my home-life was new. Venus and Ronan would make comments, little digs to poke my temper to get me to say something about how Indy and I were together. I thought the sentiment had been limited to them, but after hearing Tonya talk, apparently not. "We agreed we weren't happy, but neither of us wants anyone else. So we're working on it."

"Working on it?"

"Dating."

"You're mated," he said.

"Listen to some sage advice from your elder brother. Don't quit wooing your mate."

"Yeah, but you never wooed her in the first place."

"Exactly."

"And she's all for it? I know you said she doesn't want to be with anyone else, but she wants to be with you? Specifically?"

I hadn't been the only one with those questions. "I haven't scared her away yet."

"You won't. But are you going to let her in all the way?"

I ground my teeth together. Ronan too? What would Venus and Ronan think about what I had done? I couldn't tell them or they'd be complicit. My silence protected more than me. I had acted unlike a future clan leader. I had been impulsive, selfish, and destructive. Three traits I had sworn I would never be. And it had helped the town. I could take solace in that fact while enduring the shame hiding the truth caused.

"I'm letting her in," I said too defensively. "But we all have a part of ourselves that we don't share with anyone."

"Do we?" Ronan had never been afraid to challenge me. Even when my parents had pitted us against each other, he'd never backed down, not when he'd been younger and smaller, and definitely not now when we were equally matched. "Because I've got to tell you, I can tell Brighton anything. That's how I knew she was definitely the one. I wanted her to be the right female for me, but want and need are two different things. You need someone you can completely be yourself with."

"I am being authentic with her."

"Doesn't sound like it."

"It's in the past."

"Does it have to do with our parents?"

Could I end the conversation with a rhetorical question? "Isn't everything?"

He snorted. "I guess that's right. But hey, if you expect me to listen to you because you're an old wise one, then listen to me as the old married guy."

"Shifters don't marry."

"No, what we have goes much deeper. But you know what I mean. If four years of living with your salty ass haven't scared Indy off, then she's in this thing with you. The only obstacle you have to overcome is you."

I scowled at the papers littering the top of my desk. City invoices covered my keyboard, and I left them there so I didn't have to tackle the hundred messages in my inbox. I was still catching up from when I was gone.

"She's still with you," he said. "And don't say it's because she didn't have a choice. If Indy would've told one of her siblings she wanted to get away from you, they would've helped her. Her parents too."

That was true. Her siblings might've scattered, but it would only take one complaint from her and they'd find a way to deal with me. Whether they squirreled her away, or found a way to make me disappear, it'd happen. "Staying with me might've given her a certain level of freedom from her family." What she called smothering was a deep vein of protectiveness.

"Maybe. But like I said, there would've been other

options if they had wanted to think of some. She's with you. Don't discount that, or her."

My scowl deepened. I wasn't discounting her. She had asked me to quit underestimating her. But the secret I had was different. I would work on everything else, but I couldn't let my family and my mate know what I had done. To get Ronan off my back, I said, "Got it."

We chatted for a few more minutes. He filled me in on all things Garnet River and said Venus and Penn would head back to Jade Hills next week.

It was on the tip of my tongue to tell him about Dallas, but my office wasn't the place. Next time I talked to Ronan, I'd call him from home. The four city council members for Jade Hills had offices on the other side of the building, the way I preferred it. With shifter hearing, I didn't want to risk them overhearing suspicion about Dallas.

Three of the four members of my council had been elected after my parents' deaths, and the fourth was an elderly shifter who preferred to stay on the council to ensure history didn't repeat itself. But Dallas was slick. I didn't trust him, and I couldn't come straight out and ask each council member if they distrusted him without having to answer some questions.

"I'll talk to you later," Ronan said, and we disconnected.

I set my phone on the desktop and stared at it for a few minutes. Ronan's advice circled in my head like a seagull over a department store parking lot. Had I made the right decision?

The problem was, once the information was out in the world, it was impossible to take back. Indy was everything to me, and I refused to risk her.

~

Indy

THE TEMPERATURE CLIMBED NORTH of eighty degrees as I worked on the downed trees around the cabin. Thankfully, none of them had hit the structure. For the last six hours, I sawed and chopped and hauled. A neat stack of firewood sat by the side of the cabin for the winter when my parents liked to retreat to the woods and hike and shift. A large pile of branches sat by the chipper my brother had purchased a couple of years ago. I could use some of the mulch for the house.

I swiped the back of my wrist across my sweaty forehead. I could finish the rest in a couple of days. I glanced at my phone. There were still a couple of hours before I met Lachlan for dinner.

Squinting at the lawn that'd need mowing in a few days, the rest of the storm debris, and the weeds in the flower bed, I decided it could all wait. Our summers were short enough, I wanted to enjoy the day. I brushed my hands off, went to the water spout outside the cabin, and filled my water bottle. The trees would be cooler and the slight breeze made the day pleasurable for someone who wasn't doing manual labor.

Three different trails crossed through my parents' property, all of them mostly used by shifters. One stretched around Jade Hills and ended up on the other side of Mirror Lake. The next time I hiked there, I wanted to be with my mate.

Another trail was the same one I'd been with Dallas on. The little clearing with a pile of rocks a farmer had dumped had been where I'd finally succumbed to Dallas's charms. And where I'd wanted to hike straight to the lake, dunk myself in, and wash him right off.

The sense of wrongness had been immediate and lasting.

Would it have been that way with anyone else? Perhaps that was the reason I hadn't pursued someone. The reason Dallas had been a deliberate decision.

The wrong decision. Was it only Lachlan and Ronan who suspected him? It wasn't as if I could ask around.

The last trail trekked from the place where Lachlan's parents' house used to stand, to town. It was a good mile-and-a-half hike. I could go there and back and be home in time for a quick shower before—

My belly twirled and I smiled. If I looked in the mirror, I'd probably have a dreamy expression with a light blush. Another night in Lachlan's arms. I couldn't wait.

Taking off, I let the sun soak the ache out of my muscles from working all morning and part of the afternoon. The fatigue from getting half the sleep I normally did faded to the background as I got a second wind.

Birds sang around me, and I navigated the trail without thought. I hadn't been this relaxed in years.

I was nearing the place where Lachlan grew up. I sped up as if seeing his old home would give me perspective. As a kid, we had steered clear of the Jades. His parents had sometimes plowed through our property, wreaking havoc. Mom and Dad hadn't taken us to the cabin unless Lachlan's parents were out of town. Then after they passed, we'd had several family gatherings until my parents had quit vacationing here altogether.

I kept coming because I'd been obsessed with Lachlan

and hoped to catch a glimpse of him. I hadn't, except for that one time I'd been on a hike with Dallas after we had been together. The entire time, I'd been planning how to break up with Dallas, and after I'd seen Lachlan in his dragon form, and then later as a male glaring at both of us, my mind had been made up—there wouldn't be another time with another male until he made me flush with warmth and swamped with desire like seeing Lachlan did.

Little had I known I'd get Lachlan.

I stopped at the edge of the clearing that had once been a nightmare home for three kids. My parents had told stories about what they used to hear before they'd quit going to the cabin until it was safe. Yelling, screaming, snarling. At night, the siblings would fight until one of them fell from the sky.

Shifters were supposed to be strong. Dragon shifters were supposed to be the first to fight and the last to fall. But my mom said one night she'd cried. Lachlan and Ronan had been battling in the sky, and they'd been forced to keep fighting until it rained blood and scales.

I had remembered their story, but I hadn't thought about it recently. It seemed so far in the past that it hadn't been Lachlan. As if the male who'd learned to fight brutally dirty wasn't the one I woke up with this morning.

As I stared at the burned remnants of the house that had been left to rot, I tried to see what Lachlan was trying to leave behind. Was there something here that would tell me why he'd closed himself off from me? Did the part of himself he was keeping from me have to do with anything here?

It was just land. Blood that had been soaked into the

ground was long gone, while trees that had heard the family suffering were still standing. This place was nothing but an abandoned property with the scraps left from the fire.

Where had he buried his parents?

As part of Jade clan, we'd heard they died in an accident. The announcement came with a sense of relief, and shock that their reign was over, then nervous anticipation. What would Lachlan be like?

There hadn't been a big farewell for the older Jades. No public funeral. Half the council resigned and Lachlan had used the new shifters elected to issue a termination order on a third for crimes committed against mountain shifters. Violations his parents had been happy to ignore.

Prickles dotted the back of my neck moments before a scream ripped through the air.

I stepped back into the trees and scanned around.

Was the creature that screamed the same one that had been out the night Lachlan and I tried to picnic?

Another scream rang out, closer this time.

Were there two again?

The sun was high in the sky. We didn't have many humans using the trails around Jade Hills. The only benefit of the isolation his parents had caused. The humans in and around town were mated to shifters. Kids of shifter-human pairs were always shifters.

I waited, listening. My senses flared. Should I message Lachlan? I didn't know what I was up against. Mountain lion shifters? We didn't get too many wolf or bear shifters over the border, but it still happened, especially if they were on the run from their own shifter law.

My pulse went up another notch, my heart hammering. Lachlan's comment about fighting to kill rose in my mind.

I took out my phone, hating how typing a message took my attention away.

Hiked to your old place. Screams are happening again.

I clutched the device in my hands as I waited. Should I head back to the cabin? Undress and shift?

An acrid stench blew across my nose. Like fresh cat pee.

Mountain lion shifters. Were they feral? Lachlan had achieved a peaceful status with the surrounding packs. I couldn't see one of them starting shit with Jade Hills just because.

My phone buzzed. **OMW**

My pulse eased a notch. He was on his way. I hated to be as relieved as I was. I'd been wanting him to come to me about work stuff. I'd been wanting to be included. Yet the first incident I had and I didn't know what to do.

A low growl reached my ears.

I tossed my phone on the ground and ripped my shirt off. Next, my shorts and shoes were kicked off. Without wasting time, I shifted.

My bones elongated, a welcome relief to the tension coiled inside of me. My skin morphed into scales and my face elongated into a snout. The change barely took a few seconds, but awareness tingled over my body.

I hunkered in the trees and swung my head around. To the left, then to the right.

Two mountain lion shifters wouldn't take on a shifted dragon shifter. They could get the jump on me when I was in my human form and rip me apart. Our natural healing ability wouldn't be able to recover from the severe blood loss losing a limb would cause. We weren't immortal.

I crept along the trail. I wasn't hiding until Lachlan arrived. Enough of this. I might not know what to do, but I wasn't useless. Tree branches scraped against my scales and leaves whispered over the bony points running down my back. I went slow to keep the noise down.

My phone buzzed. I couldn't pick it up with my talon-tipped limbs. Was Lachlan trying to reach me?

Stopping, I reconsidered my path. I was heading back to the cabin, but I'd leave my clothes behind. Lachlan was coming to me. I angled around, only bumping my tail against three different trees. Once I faced the opposite direction, I lumbered toward the clearing.

A cat's scream erupted from my right.

I answered with a low rumble, refusing to roar when there could be ears that didn't need to hear close by.

Another cry from my left.

I kept my quiet growl going until I reached the remains of the house. The smell of urine and rot reached my nose. I prowled around the rectangular house foundation. The musty scent of old wood and death stained the air, but the last of ammonia made my dragon eyes water.

Urine. Definitely a big cat. The scent was easier to identify in my dragon form. I inhaled and exhaled again and again.

Mountain lion shifter, as I expected, but their scent saturated the place. That took time. A lengthy stay or a deliberate showing day after day to create this stench.

No more sounds came from the woods.

Had they been messing with me? Did I scare them off when I shifted? Feral shifters weren't rational. They didn't run when they should. They attacked for all the wrong reasons.

I crept around the remains of the house. Pieces had been piled on one side, likely to dig out the bodies and bury them. The fire had been in the middle of the night. His mom and dad had probably been in their bedroom.

I curved around one side where the highest pile of charred wood was stacked. The corner of a metal bed frame poked out from underneath the rubble. Was this their bedroom? Lachlan and the others had moved out years before the accident.

That didn't mean the other rooms couldn't still have beds.

But the area cleared was the living room.

How had Lachlan and the others known they'd be in the living room? Or had they shuffled debris around until they found them?

The soft thud of feet against the ground made me snap my head around. Lachlan's fresh rain scent reached me right as he emerged from the trail, wearing nothing but boxers. He ground to a stop when he saw me.

I dipped my head to acknowledge him. He'd been ready to shift, but if he'd run across an unwitting human, he'd just be some lost dude running through the woods. The nearby lake would help sell the story of him being in just boxers.

I shifted back, rotating my head as it felt like I was cramming a pillow into a compact. The sensation would wear off. "I haven't heard them for a few minutes, but this area smells like mountain lion shifter pee, and I think the bones of their kill are in the debris." I waved to the piles of wood behind me.

His features tightened when he glanced at the house.

"Ferals trying to find a place to squat?"

"Maybe, but I didn't catch the sour scent." Didn't mean they weren't new ferals, not quite mindless but on their way. "Think they'll come back or find a new place?"

"I don't know," he said grimly. "I have to hunt for them." Our date night would be postponed. "I'll walk you back to the cabin. Can you head straight back to the house from there?"

Damn. We were finally finding ourselves, and his work reared its head. "I can help you hunt."

"If this was a normal feral hunt, I wouldn't have a problem, but this is different."

He had nothing more to go on than a feeling, but I was getting the same sense deep in my gut. I was out on my own. Coincidence or intentional? The location of my parents' cabin and the fact that I was often there weren't a secret. If I helped Lachlan, we'd have to stay together in case I was indeed a target. I'd hinder him. He could be quicker and stealthier on his own.

"Okay."

He shot me a grateful look. "I'll turn around while you get dressed. Otherwise, I'm going to put us in a compromising position."

His confession took the sting out of missing date night with him. I dressed and grabbed my phone. The message was from my parents. **Want to come for dinner? I want to thank you for cleaning up at the cabin. Spaghetti and meatballs?**

My stomach growled. Mom's spaghetti and meatballs were legendary. Her meatballs were the size of my face. A consolation prize for being alone tonight.

"You can turn around," I said, but he didn't have to. The way his boxer briefs hugged his ass was something I hadn't seen enough of lately. When he did, I wiggled my phone. "Mom and Dad invited me over tonight."

"Good. It might be better."

"Want me to call you when I head home?"

He nodded and crossed toward me, turning me with a hand on the small of my back. "I don't know how long this will take."

"If you're done earlier than expected, come over. Mom will feed you."

He only nodded.

My parents had been thrilled when Lachlan announced he wanted me for his mate. They'd been cautious, but by then, he'd proven himself a worthy ruler. While they hadn't disliked Dallas, they'd heard all the same rumors and were cautious. Mostly, I thought they realized I wasn't crazy about him and were afraid I wouldn't be true to myself.

Being with Lachlan meant I'd stay in Jade Hills. I'd be protected since I didn't have five brothers and sisters around to do the job. Lachlan had kept his distance with them like he'd done with everyone else.

LACHLAN

I waited until dark before I shifted to my dragon and soared over the treetops. I agreed with Indy when she said she thought the mountain lion shifters had been camping at my old place.

Why the hell would they be here?

I should've cleaned up that mess long ago. I should've

lit another match and burned the rest of it to the ground. But it had served as a reminder. A monument to why I needed to do better and be better.

I peered through the treetops, flying low to see and smell better. Earlier, I had found tracks from one of them. They'd been big cat prints, and I followed them for miles.

A crumpled carcass caught my eye. I dipped between an opening between some trees and landed, folding my wings before a branch tore at the sensitive webbing.

Backtracking to the animal remains, I sniffed. It wasn't fresh, but it'd been killed earlier today and only half had been eaten. The stench of male mountain lion shifter surrounded the spot.

I was miles from the path Indy had been on, but shifters had excellent hearing. Had she interrupted the meal? Had the second shifter heard her and let out a scream to notify this one?

I wanted to know what was going on.

I wasn't getting any answers tonight.

I was supposed to be with my mate. We'd be done with dinner by now, possibly even naked. Instead, I was in my dragon form, hunting something I couldn't explain.

Why were they hanging out at my old home? The property still belonged to me, and I'd done little with it other than try to forget what went on. My parents' legacy had been strong enough to keep others away. And now, strange mountain lion shifters were hanging around, and my mate decided to take a leisurely walk here.

I should've torched the entire place when I had the chance. It wouldn't have looked suspicious then. Today was a different story. It would be obvious to others I had something to hide.

A low growl vibrated my chest. What the hell did

those shifters want?

I watched through the canopy of the trees and flew toward Indy's parents' cabin, where I had parked my pickup. Once I received Indy's text, I abandoned my work and broke every traffic law possible to get here. My discarded shirt still lay on the passenger side of the pickup. Indy must've folded up my jeans and put them on the driver's seat, also shutting the door for me.

Warmth bloomed in my chest.

Was she still at her parents' place? I hadn't seen Paul or Janet in months. I hadn't really talked to them in a couple of years. There was no animosity between us, but I hadn't fostered a relationship. They had seemed nice enough. The type of couple to take any of their children's significant others under their figurative wings. I hadn't really included myself in that category since Indy hadn't had much of a choice but to be with me.

I dressed and climbed behind the wheel. Making my decision, I turned the engine over and drove to Jade Hills, bypassing the turn that would take me to my house and headed to the other side of town.

I reached a well-kept older home on two acres of property. Too little land for six rambunctious dragon shifters, but Paul and Janet had succeeded.

Indy's car was out front, and I parked behind it in the driveway.

By the time I made my way down the short path to the front stoop, Janet was opening the door, a grin gracing her seventy-year-old face. "Lachlan, what a surprise. Indy wasn't sure you'd be able to make it."

I stuffed my hands in my front pockets and entered, wiping my shoes off on her welcome mat. "Work was getting me nowhere."

Her grin deepened and lines fanned out by each eye. Her hair had once been as dark as her daughter's but was now salt and pepper, heavy on the salt. She kept it short as if she didn't have time to mess with something so menial. Janet was a female who liked to stay busy, and doing her hair wasn't high on her priority list.

Indy poked her head out of the kitchen and did a double take. She rounded the corner in a long skirt she favored when she wasn't in shorts and a tank top. "Lachlan." Her eyebrows drew together. "Did you finish so soon?"

"That's the thing about work, it'll always wait for you."

Janet chuckled and patted my arm. "Isn't that the truth." She'd been the only person to casually touch me like that. I liked to think of her back pats as a maternal gesture, something I hadn't gotten while growing up.

Paul rounded behind her and came to shake my hand as he always did. He wore a striped polo and navy shorts with white New Balance shoes. No one would suspect he could turn into a dragon. "Thought I heard someone at the door." His grip was strong, but not like it had been four years ago.

I had always admired Indy for taking care of her family, but newfound respect ignited inside of me. Shifters aged like humans, and while we didn't suffer many of the same maladies as humans did, thanks to our natural healing abilities, time still wore us down. Indy took care of the people she loved, and one day I would be lucky to be included among them.

Janet patted me on the shoulder again as she walked by. "It just so happens I was telling Paul that I made too many meatballs. We would never be able to finish them off ourselves."

She and Paul disappeared into the kitchen. Indy crossed to me and put her hands on my chest. *"No luck?"* she mouthed.

I shook my head.

Her mouth pinched, but she didn't remove her hands. "I'm glad you came. They were asking about you. Mom's afraid you're going to work too much without Ronan."

"I'm not afraid. I know it," Janet called from the kitchen.

The corner of my mouth kicked up, and humor danced in Indy's amber eyes.

Paul popped out of the kitchen once more. "This will save us time. Did Indy tell you we were wondering what to do about the cabin?"

"No, Dad," Indy answered, her tone wry. "You only just told me tonight."

I arched a brow, but she grabbed my hand and took me to the large plank of a kitchen table rounded with eight chairs.

So many seats and there still wouldn't be enough seating for all of Indy's family. A spark of envy flared hot before being quenched with cool gratitude. I had grown up knowing what it was like to have almost no one. As an adult, I had two siblings, plus their mates. I talked to Deacon Silver enough to consider him a friend. Same with his younger brother, Steel. But Indy had been removed from all that. Yet she'd had her own, and that helped me feel like I failed my mate a little less.

The savory smell of seasoned meat rose in the air. My appetite turned from hungry to ravenous. I pulled out a chair and Indy took the one next to it.

Within minutes, a steaming plate of noodles loaded with more meatballs than I could count was slid in front of me. "This beats Griffin's any day of the week."

"Now, Lachlan." Paul chuckled. "You're going to make me blush."

I barked out a laugh and caught Paul and Janet's startled glances before they joined in. Indy scooted her chair closer and draped her arm along the back of mine. I had looked forward to my date night with Indy, but as a consolation prize, this was pretty damn good too.

I RECLINED in the same chair I had eaten the boatload of spaghetti in. My legs were stretched out and crossed at the ankles, and an ice-cold beer rested on the top of the table.

I was digesting Paul and Janet's idea about the cabin. "You want to make a resort?"

"A shifter resort," Janet clarified. "For camping. That Indy will run."

"We know it's only one cabin," Paul said. "But we're thinking about how to expand."

I glanced at Indy. I didn't want her to think I didn't have faith in her. She split her time between the salon and helping her parents. Overall, the cabin required only a few days a month, depending on inclement weather. Was this what she wanted to do?

Would she be able to?

"I'd be the manager," Indy said. "I'd hire on for cleaning and maintenance once we have a couple more."

"We don't go to the woods very often these days." Janet folded her hands on top of the table next to the glass of rosé. "The kids are all self-sufficient, and we don't want Indy to feel beholden to us. We also don't want to sell and no longer have the property in our family. The land has been in our family for generations."

And they'd kept it with my parents living next door. "Have you thought about how to market to just shifters?" The last thing I needed was to be approached with discrimination lawsuits. The excuse that the renters weren't human would go very far.

"We've been thinking about that." Paul spun his empty beer bottle between his fingers. "We can make it look like a time-share, or the only advertising we do is word-of-mouth between Jade Hills, Silver Lake, Gemstone, and Penopal. Ronan could let Garnet and Peridot clan know. But if we do this, it'll be revenue for you and Indy to grow your hoard for your family."

Janet and Paul leveled their steady gazes on me and Indy.

Our family. We had talked about kids. I wanted to see her belly swell with my child more than anything, but I refused to be selfish about it. I had to earn her trust as a mate first. Then her trust in me as a father would come next.

What would I be like as a parent? I had shitty role models. I'd never been around children. Babies might as well be an alien life form. I hadn't even met Steel and Avril's baby girl. Having and raising a family terrified me, but I was good at lining my priorities up and ignoring ones that were too far down the line.

The first priority was the couple and my mate staring hopefully at me. "You'd need a business permit issued by the city. It has to be a legitimate company. Everything by the book. Jade Hills can't afford to fall under fire for cabin rentals that only rent to certain people."

It would be a PR nightmare. A shifter PR nightmare. No little shifter town had hotels. We didn't have businesses that encouraged humans to visit and stay for longer than lunch. Our diners wouldn't turn humans away, but at least they were in public. Jade Hills was small enough to know who were strangers and who wasn't. Travelers weren't an unusual occurrence. Vacationers with no other ties to the shifter world were. And they were dangerous.

"I think it would work," Indy said. "It would give me something to do."

"The salon?" I gave her a look that asked her what she'd said about working with me.

"Working with Venus was also just something to do. I don't mind giving manicures or pedicures, but I'm continuing to do it to help Venus and to see clients like Edna. Venus is getting more entrenched with Penn and setting up the online education systems, so I don't plan on leaving." She curled her hand around mine and gave it a quick squeeze. Both of her parents tracked the movement. We normally weren't a PDA couple. "And I know you're willing to bring me into your office, and I'd like to help, but knowing you're willing to means a lot. I want to find something I'm passionate about and the cabin has been a place where I've collected my thoughts and found peace. If I can do that for others..." She lifted a shoulder and released my hand.

She wanted to help people. Help the town, like she was doing with Venus and Edna. When I didn't come to her about work and her role as my mate, she thought she was cut off from an avenue where she had a role.

Venus's salon had become an integral business in Jade Hills. Money from the town flowed through its businesses and back to the people. Since my parents had died, people had been willing to open coffee shops, insurance agencies, and even boutiques downtown.

Indy and her family wanted to do the same. They were looking to benefit the town with what they already owned. It was a good idea, but we were shifters, and we had to be careful.

Indy rested her hand on my forearm, her warmth seeping into my skin. "There's a lot to think about and more to talk about. We don't have to decide tonight."

"Not at all," Paul said. "I know how you like to think about things, and we're not rushing you."

"I appreciate it." I stared at a drop of condensation running down the side of the beer bottle. The three of them had been eager to tell me about the idea. The plan was fledgling at best, but it had promise. It needed to be done right, and I was afraid I'd give them the impression I had kicked the prop away from the door to close in their face. "I'll think about it. If there's a way to make it happen, we'll find it."

Indy gave me a small smile. I hadn't said yes, but I had listened. These were the moments I missed Ronan. We'd toss ideas back and forth in my office. I didn't have him, but maybe Venus and Penn would have insight.

"Is Ronan putting his house up for sale?" Janet grabbed Paul's empty beer bottle and her wineglass to take them to the kitchen. As she went, she said, "Darren —you remember my second oldest son—and his mate were considering moving back to Jade Hills instead of Gemstone. The house they're in now is small, and my daughter-in-law's due in a few months." The grin she aimed my way was pure delight. "Isn't that exciting? My third grandchild."

Paul's grin was equally thrilled. "He was asking about Ronan's place. I know you can't play favorites, but if Ronan's not planning to sell, I can pass that information along to Darren so they can look elsewhere."

"The house is Ronan's private property. If he wants to sell to someone specific, it's not the town's business."

Janet blinked as if she was surprised I would be willing to encourage Ronan to deal directly with her son. "Oh, we'd appreciate it. They're good kids. Responsible too, or I wouldn't recommend them."

"I can send him a message now." I was driven by an urge to please Paul and Janet just because. They were good people and good parents. If this was the way I could acknowledge my appreciation for them, I was happy to do it.

I punched in a message to Ronan. It was after ten, and if he was in bed with his mate, his phone was the last thing on his mind.

"Can I ask you something?" Janet hovered at the edge of the cupboards between the kitchen and the dining room. She was wringing her hands.

Caution stole into my awareness. Janet powered her way through life, but a subject she wanted to talk to me about made her cautious? They had been my parents' longest-lasting neighbors. Had they heard something? Seen something that fateful night?

"Yes." Tension stole across my shoulders. Indy cocked her head as if she was unaware of what her mother was talking about.

Janet held up a finger and rushed down the hallway, saying, "Just a minute."

Paul looked as if he was biting back a smile. I exchanged a glance with Indy, but she shook her head. I'd like to think Janet's change in demeanor had nothing to do with me, but it obviously did, yet Paul was trying not to grin.

Janet came out with three skeins of yarn in her hands. "Do you like these colors?"

I stared at the cream, brown, and green yarn.

"Or maybe I should ask, what's your favorite color?" Janet shuffled the skeins in various orders, turning one lengthwise as if she was deciding how they looked the best.

"I..." I'd never been asked what my favorite color was. No one cared if I had a favorite food. Favorite song, favorite movie, favorite T-shirt, it didn't matter. I answered honestly. "I don't know."

"You don't know what your favorite color is?" Janet sounded surprised.

"I've never thought about it."

Indy gave my arm a reassuring squeeze, and I hadn't realized I needed her steadying touch until then.

"Oh." Janet assessed the colors.

Paul changed the way she had them arranged to put them in the order of cream, green, brown. They probably had fancier names than that, but I would be the last to guess what their real color names were. The green was light, like a jade stone. Probably a popular yarn in Jade Hills. The brown wasn't as deep as the bark of a tree, but more like the color of the clay underneath the black soil in our area. And the cream, well, it was just cream. Nice colors. I had no other opinions about them.

"The colors are fine." I had to be able to answer at least one of her questions tonight.

She beamed and adjusted the skeins as if they had to be perfectly aligned before she made whatever decision she was asking me about. "I'd like to make you a blanket."

"Why?"

Indy twined her fingers through mine. "Mom's crocheted a blanket for all of us. You know the emerald green and black one on the guest room bed?"

The blanket Indy referred to had been draped over a chair in our old bedroom. In the new house, she had put it on the guest room bed she slept in. Had she not used it on our bed, unsure of what I would think?

"I know the one," I said.

"That's the one she made for me. And she's made one for my brothers and sisters and their mates."

"And for our grandkids," Paul added, pride shining in his eyes.

Janet hooked her hands together in front of her, the nerves from earlier gone. "After you and Indy mated, I picked up the colors, and I had an idea of the pattern, but I just..." She let her hands drop. "I didn't know if you'd like it. But I'm afraid I'm going to crochet you one anyway."

She was going to make me a blanket? I didn't know anything about knitting or crocheting other than they took time. They were often projects people made for themselves or their loved ones. The care and consideration that went into them humbled me.

"No one's ever made anything for me before." I fought to keep the rawness out of my voice.

"It's my pleasure, really." Janet tapped her finger on each skein of yarn. "Paul, I do believe that is how the colors line up the best."

"You ever get time off, son?" Paul asked, both saving

me with a subject change and catching me off guard. It was amazing I didn't topple out of my chair with the way my head spun.

I'd never been called son in my life. Bastard was one of the more pleasant names. "I'd like to say yes, but my time in Garnet River made it more of a work trip." Suddenly, those pictures and rumors of me and Memphis bothered me. They were bullshit, but did Paul and Janet know? I wasn't interested in Memphis, and the sentiment was the same for her. "Other than visiting my brother, there was no personal reason for my trip. I swear."

Dragons didn't make oaths lightly. Breaking them was worth a termination order. One of the rules to keep our secrets ours.

"Indy told us." His scowl wasn't aimed at me. "Shame people gotta try to make rotten milk out of fresh cream."

"I agree. I wouldn't have mated if I wasn't serious about your daughter, sir." It seemed four years too late to ease their worries. "Ronan was more than capable of ruling this clan. It's insulting to me as much as Indy when people spread rumors about us."

Janet dropped into her chair. "I thought the same, but I can't tell you how much it means to us to hear you say it. Indy is our baby. We want all our kids happy, but sometimes it's easy to convince ourselves lightning can't strike six times."

I was determined to be the sixth lightning strike in their lives. I had been territorial over my mate before, but after tonight with her family, I was more determined than ever to protect what was mine. Because tonight, they had made me feel like one of them.

EIGHT

I ndy

LACHLAN LEFT his pickup out for the night, and I pulled into the garage. When I climbed out, I shut my door, and Lachlan roamed around the perimeter of the house. It wasn't unusual for him to wander outside at night. Restless energy built up inside of him sitting at a desk all day. He didn't have to tell me; it was obvious.

Tonight was the first time I joined him. "Is everything okay? I know my parents can be a lot."

They had taken it easy on Lachlan. Always had. Mom was the neighborhood mom. My siblings brought friends to our house. Their mates were immediately welcomed into the fold. But they hadn't been sure how Lachlan would react to their special form of smothering. They'd had a front-row seat into too much of his abominable treatment.

Mom and Dad were extreme extroverts, and they loved people. The more, the merrier, and that included kids, their mates, grandkids, friends, and acquaintances. They enjoyed gatherings and gifting and socializing of any sort.

The exact opposite of Lachlan and his family. Venus had opened up since she had mated Penn, but the couple still kept to themselves. They were friendly enough, but their social circle comprised mostly their siblings and mates. I suspected Ronan would be the same.

"Your parents aren't a lot." His footsteps were soft on the thick grass. "I wanted to make sure I didn't sense any shifters spying on us."

A chill stole over my skin. This was my home. No one was going to make me feel unsafe here. "Do you have any idea what's going on?"

He shook his head. "All I know is that it's something. And you and I are involved."

"Why would mountain shifters camp out in your parents' old place? I get that it's abandoned, but you feel like there's more going on. Is it personal, or are they targeting Jade?"

He shrugged and kept his casual pace wandering around the yard. "It's very possible a grudge from a long time ago that's festered. I can't think of anything recent."

"But why your parents' place?" I slowed to a stop, hoping he didn't continue his meandering path without me.

He took a few more steps, finally coming to a halt. He shoved his hands in the pockets of his jeans and dropped his head. "There's a lot about my history I don't know that I'll ever talk about."

Hearing him admit that he didn't want to talk to me sent a spiral of hurt through my belly.

Was I being unfair? If I had grown up the way he had, would I want to revisit the trauma just to appease my mate? Shifters went to therapists. Shifters became therapists. But Lachlan wasn't the type to be comforted by talking. Maybe someday, he'd be comforted by talking to me. Yet if he had dealt with what had happened to him growing up, he might not need to recount the stories and work through his emotions.

"I'm not going to expect you to. It wouldn't be fair."

"Indy..." He kept his back to me for several moments before slowly turning around. "There's something specific I don't know that I'll ever be able to talk about."

I closed the distance between us and cupped my hands around his face. "Is it something you *need* to talk to me about?"

His gaze was conflicted, and he appeared to be thinking about his answer. What had happened? If he had worked through his childhood, then what continued to haunt him? And why? Was he afraid of losing himself, or me?

He answered my unspoken question. "I don't know. I'm afraid that if I tell you, I'll lose you, and I'm afraid if anyone else finds out, I'll lose everything else." His admission kept me rooted in place. Lose me? Lose everything? It didn't make sense. "Were you unfaithful?"

He recoiled, nearly jerking his face out of my hands. Then he gripped his palms around my wrists. "I would never betray you like that. Ever since I saw you, you're the only one I've wanted."

How could this gruff, hard male say the sweetest things? "Then you won't lose me. But I'm not going to push you, Lachlan. I want you to talk to me when you're ready."

"What if I'm never ready?"

He was ashamed. He had done something he regretted—no. I didn't get the sense he regretted what had happened but feared how the information might affect him and the ones he loved.

"I think one day you will be," I finally said. I brushed my hands down to his strong shoulders. "And I'll still be here, ready to accept whatever news you have to give me."

"God, Indy, I don't deserve you."

"I think you deserve a lot more than you think." I rose to my tiptoes and brushed a kiss across his lips. Then I tucked my arms through his, and we continued walking across the yard.

The moon was a sliver above us and stars dotted the night sky. Thin clouds floated in the air, a fine curtain low above the horizon. Overhead, the Milky Way was visible thanks to the lack of light pollution this far from town.

"The stars are gorgeous," I said it more to let him know it was okay our earlier conversation was done. We had made so much progress in such a short amount of time. I wanted to give him the same space he had given me for four years.

"There are supposed to be falling stars visible tonight and tomorrow." He changed direction to start leading me toward the driveway.

I was disappointed this peaceful moment would be over, but I looked forward to crawling into bed with him again. "I haven't seen a falling star in forever."

When we reached the pickup, he didn't veer toward the door of the house. He dropped the tailgate and lifted me to sit on it. I crossed my ankles and braced my hands on the end of the tailgate. He folded his arms and leaned next to me.

"I always wish I knew more about constellations at times like this." I tipped my head back, gazing at the cloud of stars streaking over the sky, making up our galaxy. "Do you think our ancestors knew about constellations?"

"They used the sun, the moon, and the stars to navigate, but I doubt they attributed any mythology to pictures they thought the stars made. They would have been too arrogant for that."

I chuckled and slowly kicked my feet back and forth. "I can't imagine spending all our time in dragon form. Can you imagine how they mated then?" My cheeks burned.

"I don't think there's a dragon shifter alive who doesn't imagine how our ancestors had dragon sex."

I laughed, the sound rolling across the lawn to fade. "Maybe that's the real reason they made the trade with the witches and wizards to turn into dragon shifters. More orgasms."

The corner of his mouth ticked up and starlight danced in his green eyes. "From everything we've learned about the original dragons, I believe that would've been a huge motivation."

I nudged his side with my knee. "I can't blame them."

He flipped around. I uncrossed my feet so he could wedge between my knees. Sitting like this, I was face-to-face with him. A little sway forward and my lips were pressed to his. The warm air of the night only made me more aware of the heat rising in my body, swirling until it pooled between my legs.

Last night had been amazing, exhilarating. I would love to do it again, in any way, shape, or form. But at the same time, it wasn't enough.

He was open with me tonight. Honest. Would I hold out, keeping us from both getting what we wanted, just because I wanted all his secrets?

That didn't seem right.

He was my mate, and I wanted to be with him. After the last week, the need had only grown, and it had nothing to do with biological urges. I wanted this male. Lachlan Jade. My mate.

"Lachlan," I murmured against his lips. "I want you."

"I know, baby. I'll give it to you."

I dropped my hands to the waistband of his pants. "No. I want all of you. I want us to be together tonight."

He paused, blinking at me, his hands around my thighs and his powerful erection had already built up behind his waistband. My fingertips were so close, but I waited for him to give me his answer to a question I hadn't asked.

This wasn't just about me. This was about us. I was ready. Was he?

LACHLAN

"You wanted to wait." My brain was having a hard time trying to be logical. Doing the right thing had never been so hard.

"I wanted you to talk to me. To be honest with me. And you were." Her fingers tightened around my waistband, and I felt that the same as if she had given my dick a pump.

I had been honest by telling her I wasn't ready to talk to her and that I may never be ready.

"I understand, Lachlan. You were still open with me, and I appreciate it."

"You don't have to sleep with me to show me your gratitude."

"You're such a good male. I want to be with you because you're my mate. I want you to be my mate, and I want us to have a full life together. If we both want to have sex, then let's do it. It's not something I'm holding hostage in order to get my way. You've already given me everything you're able to."

Her words finally sank in. It was like the ocean rushed between my ears as adrenaline surged through my veins and my erection became more demanding than ever. I didn't want to take her inside and delay what we both wanted any longer. Her desire was curling around me, her honeysuckle scent teasing my nose.

I had to have her now.

She must've felt the exact moment my restraint broke. She ripped open the clasp of my pants and freed my erection. The fabric of my shirt pulled over my sensitive flesh, and with a growl, I ripped it off and tossed it on the driveway.

She had changed from her denim shorts to a long, loose skirt before she had gone to her parents'. I rolled that off her in seconds and dragged her ass to the end of the tailgate. She wrapped her arms around my neck, need straining her features. She clamped her legs around my waist and lifted herself until her hot, wet entrance hovered above the tip of my cock.

I willed myself to slow down, but she had different ideas. With the flex of her thighs, she was taking me deep. A simultaneous groan left us both. Her body clamped around mine until I knew nothing about the world around us. The croak of the frogs faded along with the rustling of the light breeze through the leaves of the trees. An entire pack of mountain lion shifters could stroll through the yard behind me, and I wouldn't notice. Because I was inside my mate.

This was different than before. Being with Indy had always been a pleasure so intense my mind threatened to explode with my body. But this time, she was a tether, holding me close to her. We weren't two separate beings seeking gratification. We were a unit. A couple.

She was the female I was in love with. I had never told her, and maybe I should have before now.

"Oh, Lachlan," she moaned, and her ass flexed until she rose up and relaxed to bring her back down my length.

My vision blurred. Fuck—how could that feel so good?

I had thought of waiting, worried it would ruin the moment, but the words rolled off my tongue. "I love you, Indy."

She stopped riding me, her hooded eyes flying wide.

Oh, shit, I wrecked it. Dammit. She wanted honesty, but maybe she hadn't been ready for *that*.

"I love you too, Lachlan." She tightened her arms around me. Her body pulsed around my dick, and for a second, I saw double. "Oh, god. I've been wanting to admit that forever, but I felt foolish."

As soon as she had said the words, I gripped her ass with my hands and encouraged the steady rhythm she had been setting with her legs. After telling her I loved her so freely, the next words were hard to say, but only because I was trying not to explode before she came all over me. "I won't ever make you feel foolish for loving me."

She let out a cry and flung her head back. My only regret was that I hadn't taken the time to rip her tank top off. Those firm little handfuls were hidden from my view.

"I've had it bad for you for so long," she gasped. She gripped my shoulders with her hands, her body going tight. "Lachlan?"

I planted my feet on the ground, refusing to fall during the explosion that was going to rock us both. "Come with me, Indy."

As if she had needed my permission, she yelled my name, silencing the crickets and frogs I had ignored as soon as she had touched me. I came with my own roar and finished bumping into her greedy body until I was empty.

It was a miracle I didn't collapse under the onslaught of ecstasy. Hearing her tell me she loved me and admitting it myself—tonight was our first real time together.

She was resting her head in the crook of my neck and trailing her fingers over my chest and abs. "If anyone was spying, they sure got an eyeful."

I tightened my embrace as irrational rage woke the overprotective male inside of me. No one was allowed to intrude on my private time with my mate. Fucking no one.

I didn't think anyone was spying on us, but I didn't want to take the chance that any more of our intimacy could be witnessed.

Gently, I lifted her off me, mourning the loss of her

heat, and held her until she was steady on the ground. Then I crowded her with my body as I picked up her skirt and helped her step in it.

When I straightened, she was frowning. "Do you think someone saw us?"

"I don't know, but I don't want to take any chances with your privacy."

She brought my head down to give me a solid kiss on my lips. "I like when you're protective of me for all the right reasons."

She had talked to me before about how my lack of communication made her feel like I doubted her abilities. "If you want to work in my office with me, I'll tell you what duties I need help on. And if you'd rather run a shifter camping resort, I'll make it fucking happen."

"We'll see." She tucked herself into my side, and I shut the tailgate. "Maybe it's time I figure out what I want to be when I grow up instead of thinking others should figure it out for me."

"You have a lot of people who want you in their lives, but I'm sure your parents feel the same way as me. We want you to do whatever makes you happy. Don't make your decisions based on what you think we need out of you. I'm not going to be the one holding you back."

I stooped to grab my shirt and then led her into the house.

"You weren't holding me back. I was. The entire time. It wasn't my siblings or my parents. I let the excuses get to me, but really I don't know." She shrugged and let her arms hang. We faced each other inside the door of our house, not going farther. "Do you think I could be a business owner?"

"Of course."

Disbelief rippled over her face as if my lack of hesitation shocked her. "I would be getting everything from my parents."

"Some people will make you feel bad for what's been given to you, but it's really none of their damn business. They have just as many judgments and assumptions about those who grew up with nothing. You're going to be judged no matter what. So do what fulfills you."

"Does being a leader fulfill you? I know it's your birthright. You had no choice. But you don't seem happy."

"I'm content. I get to help fix what generations of my family have destroyed. My brother and sister are safe, and I have you. And the more we do this"—I trailed my finger from her shoulder over her breasts and down her belly—"the happier I am."

A sexy grin lit her face. "Well, then, let's do it some more."

Above us, a shooting star soared across the sky.

NINE

I ndy

I SAT in the office next to Lachlan's and pored over city ordinances and policies. I didn't want to put my mate in a difficult situation, so I had to research how best to carry out the marketing plans for the camping resort. As a private company, we'd have a lot of leeway, and by we, it was just me.

Two weeks had passed since my parents had approached Lachlan and me with their idea, and they had made it clear they would help with brainstorming and money, but the rest would be left up to me. My siblings all had their own jobs, and this was basically my inheritance. They had seen how much I took care of the cabin, but they'd also seen beneath that. I enjoyed caring for the place. I liked making it look nice. The work gave me purpose.

Once the other two cabins were built and up and running, it wouldn't consume as much of my time. But we hadn't come out of the planning stage. First, I had to make sure our plans were feasible, and next, I had to find land for the other two cabins.

Lachlan sauntered through the doorway, an orange drink in his hand. He set it on the desk. "Are you ready for lunch?"

"You brought me a drink."

"Eh, you can guzzle it. But I ran by Lacey's, and I know you love her peach lemonade."

I took a long pull, closing my eyes as the sweet flavor hit my tongue. "How'd you know?"

"You don't get that orgasm look with every beverage."

I sputtered and coughed, shaking my head. "You're incorrigible." I handed him the cup, and he took a drink. I finished the rest.

He had asked an hour ago if I wanted to go to Griffin's for a bite to eat, and my stomach reminded me that I'd been hungry then. But diving into the history of this town was fascinating. "Did you know there is still a law on the books that says poultry isn't allowed within city limits?"

"As long as the birds aren't annoying, we don't enforce it."

"Why don't you change it?"

He lifted a shoulder. "Had a lot of other things going on. It's a minor law that no one cares to make a complaint about."

A town that had faced difficult economic times for decades didn't hold the ability to grow one's own food against anyone. "There are a lot of really petty laws still in the books."

"Some of them don't make any sense," he agreed.

I scratched the side of my head with the pen I'd been using to jot down notes. "What about if I made a list of all the ones that didn't serve Jade Hills so you and the council could do what you need to do with them?"

"I wouldn't say no." There was surprise in his tone. "Do you want, like, a formal position?"

"No. It'll be my own form of community service. I'm not deciding whether they're right or wrong. I'm just giving you the ones that don't make sense anymore while I'm going through my own stuff."

He wandered in and pressed his fingertips onto the top of the desk, peering over the papers I had scattered over the surface. "Have you found anything that would prevent you from building?"

"No. My next step is to go online and look at other business marketing plans. How can I drill down to the people I actually want to be my customers?" I ran my hand over a couple of the binders I had just gone through. "It'd be so much easier if I could just get a sign that said no humans allowed."

"Tell me about it. The Crockers wanted to turn three of their old grain bins into a trendy bed-and-breakfast, but they couldn't figure out how to keep humans from making reservations." He pushed off the desk and crossed his arms. "I kept trying to help them figure out a way. There was nothing in all our city documents I could find that would restrict a B&B, but they couldn't figure out how to keep our town's secret safe and run the business."

The Crockers were a couple in their fifties. The grain bin idea was cool, and a bed-and-breakfast would help bring a lot of shifters to town. Families, like my siblings, that had moved away but still had family in Jade Hills. Shifters from different colonies who were nosy and wanted to visit. It wasn't good for our kind to be isolated. We needed to meet mates in other clans to keep our population going. Wolf, bear, and mountain lion shifters had an easier time living and blending among the humans. Dragon shifters needed to stay in one community. It was a lot harder to hide a dragon than a mountain lion.

"Yeah, that's where it all starts to get complicated. The reservation system." An idea sparked deep in my brain. The glow grew stronger until I jumped out of my chair. "The reservation system. Maybe Penn could help."

Lachlan arched a brow. "He'd be happy to help with any of the tech stuff."

Excitement swelled in my chest. "Exactly. The tech side. That's the key. We don't need brochures, or pamphlets, or even a fancy website. All I would need is a private page for people to make reservations on. In order to get that page, they'd already be vetted as a shifter family, or-or..." I fluttered my hand around. "I don't know, but I'll think of something."

Pride lightened the shade of his eyes. "I knew you would. Do you want to stay and brainstorm or go get some lunch?"

I pressed a hand against my stomach. If I stayed to work, the rumbling would be too distracting. "Let's go eat."

I abandoned my research and walked outside with Lachlan. He nodded to people passing us. Vern, the postal carrier, gave us each a surprised smile. Lynette and Mike, who owned the Laundromat and car wash, waved from across the street. And Zoe, one of the city council members, shouted a greeting from her car as she passed.

"It's almost like being a celebrity," I said.

"It's really good to see."

The changes had been gradual but significant and, I hoped, permanent.

When we reached Griffin's, there was a young man working instead of Tonya. His eyes widened like we were actually celebrities. He scrambled to grab two menus and swallowed hard. "Hello, welcome to Griffin's. I'm Porter, and I'll be your host today."

I bit back a smile. His formality and his nerves were endearing.

"Porter... Charbonneau?" Lachlan asked.

Peter didn't relax, but he smiled at Lachlan's easy tone. "Yes, Stephanie and Mitch."

"How are they doing with that property they just bought by the lake?"

Mom and Dad gave me updates on all the goings-on in town. I struggled to recall any details, but last month she told me Porter's parents had purchased land on the other side of the lake Lachlan and I had tried to picnic at.

"They just broke ground," Porter answered. "They've saved for years for their retirement home."

"If they need anything, tell them they can just stop in."

"Absolutely. Will do, sir."

My mouth twitched again. Porter couldn't have been more than seventeen. He wouldn't remember much about life under the former ruler, but his parents would. I hoped they knew Lachlan was serious about helping them.

He placed us at a booth, one away from where we were the last time we were here. Two of the employees at the bank were seated in the booth we had been in before.

Lachlan was waiting for me to sit, but I waved for him

to go ahead. "I'm going to use the restroom. I'll be right back."

I rushed through the dining room to the long hallway that led to the bathrooms. A male emerged from one of the restrooms, and his gaze landed right on me.

"Dallas." What a coincidence. Again. "Lunch for your mama again?" Why did I seem to be running into him all the time?

After I had told him I was mating Lachlan, he'd been furious—on my behalf, though now I couldn't help but wonder. He'd been indignant that our ruler could point his finger and order me to mate him.

Not many rulers did that these days, but Lachlan had, and I hadn't minded. I'd held my triumph close to my chest, and it'd dwindled to ash each year after I'd mated him. Only a spark survived. It'd been fanned over the last week, and the flame of exhilaration burned fiercely inside me.

If yesterday was any indication of our future together, I couldn't wait to live life with him.

"No—ah, yes, but I came to chat with Porter." Dallas sold insurance at the company he'd taken over for his mom. It wouldn't be unusual for him to roam through town doing business. "Have you eaten yet? I can keep you company."

"I'm here with Lachlan."

Displeasure rippled over his features. "Those dates… must've turned out well?"

"Yes. The hike was—well, we've been able to talk, date or not. We do live together," I said like I was telling a joke.

Dallas's dour expression didn't change. "You've been talking?"

Did he mean it as a question or a flat statement? I kept my tone light. "We are mates."

"I'm more aware of that than most."

There had to be a reason why I'd been running across Dallas and thinking about how things ended between us. Perhaps one or both of us needed closure. I should've been up front with him from the beginning. "I should admit something I was too afraid to admit when we were seeing each other."

His interest turned fully on me, and I resisted the urge to squirm. When we dated, his full attention had been disconcerting, and with my inexperience, I had thought it was attraction. Nerves because I'd been into him. The reason was clear now. Distrust. I couldn't tell what he was thinking, nor did I trust he had my best interest at heart. He'd been raised as an entitled male by his abrasive mother.

She had liked me well enough until I'd become Lachlan's mate. Then she'd glared at me if we crossed paths. If I saw her car at the grocery store, I waited to go in.

"I wanted to mate Lachlan. So his proclamation wasn't a hardship." It'd been a dream come true, if a few years late in reality.

"You..." A red flush crept up his neck. "You wanted to be with him?" He enunciated each word.

"I'm sorry. Things were drawing to a close with us, and Lachlan made the announcement before I could have the talk with you."

"Drawing to a close. You never said..." He shook his head. "You were a coward."

I recoiled. "I didn't want to hurt you."

"So you kept me hoping for years that we might still have a chance?"

"I never gave you any indication I wanted to reignite what we had. And Lachlan and I didn't give any indication that we'd decided on an open relationship."

"Except him fucking around with Memphis Peridot." Dark clouds gathered in his eyes and his energy changed as if there was a subtle vibration caused by his rage.

A month ago, I would've attributed his emotion to indignation on my behalf. That was no longer the case. "He spoke with her about work, but it's not his problem, or hers, that others thought they were messing around when they were seen doing nothing more than talking to each other."

"Don't be stupid."

I clenched my hands into fists. How much trouble would I get my mate into if I decked Dallas in a public establishment? "Don't be insulting."

"He's a male used to getting whatever he wants. The females he's been with have all had experience. How do you think you could satisfy a male like that? Jades only care about themselves."

Was he talking about Lachlan and his family, or the clan as a whole? "That's none of your business. Don't talk to me again, Dallas."

I spun before I did something like kick him in the nuts —my brothers' top advice for facing an irrational male. I hadn't cleared the hallway before he caught up with me. He went to close his fingers around my arm, but I flung him off.

"Shit, Indy. I'm sorry. I just want to talk."

A wall of heat slammed into my back.

"You try touching her again, I'll remove your fingers one by one and stuff them in your hallowed out tongue." Lachlan sounded more dangerous than I'd ever heard.

Shivers traced down my spine and they had nothing to do with fear.

Dallas blanched and held his hands up. "My bad. She broke my heart all over again, and I lost my good sense."

Lachlan didn't move.

"It was a momentary lapse," Dallas kept trying to explain.

My mate's eyes narrowed. "Don't talk to her again."

I shot Lachlan a quelling glare. "I'll decide who I talk to, but I think our friendship has run its course, Dallas."

His attempt at charm slipped and I glimpsed the rage stoked in his gaze as he faced Lachlan. "I only want what's best for her."

"And what is that? Exactly?" Lachlan's voice was as sharp as a butcher knife.

"Whatever I decide." I slipped my arm through my mate's and dragged him away from the hallway.

"I overstepped," he murmured so only I could hear.

"No. Well, almost. But we needed to be a united front."

"We'll have to stay united. This might've only set him off."

I thought of Lily and how no one had seen her for years. A dragon shifter couldn't abandon their kind. A termination order would be issued if she was found. The council would've asked Lachlan to hunt for her if they thought she was alive.

As I slid into the booth, I thought about how Lachlan might've saved my life when he'd demanded I mate with him, and I'd never been so grateful he'd chosen me.

L achlan

"Wow, you're actually calling me." I could picture Ronan's shit-eating grin as he spoke. "What the hell's going on?"

"I need to talk to you about something." I watched out my kitchen window. The tree line was empty. Squirrels darted through the yard, and two tabby kittens I'd never seen before inspected the birdbath Indy had gotten from her parents after we moved in.

Indy was working at the cabin. I hated to have her out there alone, but she'd chafe under my watchful eye, and the town would suspect I didn't think she was capable. It'd only get ugly for her. As a united front, we were strong, but there were others who'd drive a wedge in any perceived weakness.

Shifters like Dallas.

Recalling the insulting way he spoke to Indy yesterday made me want to strip down and shift. He was lucky he'd been in a public place. A building, no less, where I couldn't shift.

I should've challenged him.

But again, it'd look like Indy couldn't take care of herself, and as my mate, that'd only bring her trouble.

"What's going on?" Ronan's question wasn't teasing this time.

"What do you remember of Lily and Dallas?"

"That he probably killed her because she broke up with him. Why?"

I told him about what was going on.

"Do you think the mountain lion shifters are linked to Dallas?" he asked.

"It'd be a reach, but he's shifty as hell. And the way we pissed him off last night is probably worse than what Lily would've made him feel."

"You think he has it out for Indy?"

"If he can't have her…" I wanted to kill him and get it over with, but I had to deal with him by the book. I promised myself I'd do better. People around me depended on it. "He was waiting for us to fail, and now that he knows we won't, he's going to do something. I just don't know what."

"I don't remember Lily that well. She liked to hike around the lake."

The lake. It wasn't far from the house. Indy's family's cabin was farther away, but trails wound between the shore and the cabin. Then there was my parents' place and the land I owned along the shoreline. "You think the lake has something to do with her disappearance?"

"That's the only place I ever saw her outside of town.

If you wanted to make someone disappear, that'd be a good place."

"It'd be too risky. The lake isn't deep enough to hide a body for years, and too many people fish in it and hike around it."

"Then maybe he dumped her body off one of the trails. Or he ate her."

I grimaced. "Cannibalism seems a stretch, even for him." Dallas oozed a slick salesman vibe. He dressed the opposite of me. Slacks. Polos. Loafers.

"Desperate times. I got nothing when it comes to the mountain lion shifter connection though. He might've hired them for something."

"And if I find out why, then I'd have a shit ton of answers."

"Yep."

I'd circled back into a wall. I wouldn't quit until I learned what Dallas was up to. "How's Brighton and Venus?"

"Attached at the hip. I haven't spent as much time with Penn as I have in the last week. You'd think we were the newly mated couple."

I chuckled, but a sense of loss tugged at my chest. I'd miss Ronan around. Penn and I weren't as close. He had Venus, and there was no Brighton in Jade Hills.

"He said they're leaving in a few days."

"It'll be nice to have them back. I need to talk to Penn."

"Problems?"

I told him about the camping resort idea.

He let out a whistle. "That'd be good for the town. For all shifter towns. We can get out without having to hide ourselves. If anyone can figure out how to keep it shifter only, it'll be Penn."

We wrapped up our conversation and disconnected. I stared out the window. The two kittens were creeping toward the bath where a sparrow fluttered in the water.

The bird flew away, and one kitten attacked the other.

I pushed away from the window and grabbed a couple of bowls from the cupboard. Minutes later, I was walking across the yard with one bowl full of water and the other full of tuna.

Indy hated tuna, but I'd lived off it until I'd mated her. Then she'd stocked the kitchen with more protein sources or cooked fresh tuna. If I went to the store, I still bought packets. They were my lunch and as I ate straight from the pouch, I wondered what Indy would've had instead if we'd been the type to have lunch together.

Now, I could just ask her.

The kittens raced toward the trees, but I made kissing sounds. I had no idea why, but it wasn't like they were shifters. We couldn't have a conversation.

"I, uh, have some shit for you." I set the bowls at the base of the birdbath and walked away. I stopped after several steps.

I'd never had pets. I instinctively knew what my parents would do. My siblings had been tools to use against me. Pets would be worse, and they couldn't fight back like Venus and Ronan.

The kittens crouched down and watched me. Jade Hills used to have a stray dog problem until I'd taken over. I'd given some of my parents' hoard to Zoe and told her to organize the council. They'd hired a vet to treat and spay or neuter each one, then they found good homes.

Cats hadn't been as much of an issue because of the

dogs. And with the vet we'd hired, the townsfolk had used their services. Still, litters got dumped. These two might've run away, or they might've found their way here off the main road a half mile away.

I folded my legs and dropped to my ass in the grass.

The kittens watched me, and I looked everywhere but toward them. Slowly, they made their way closer, the smell of tuna in the air too intoxicating to resist. Once they found the food, I was their last concern. They ate with loud smacks and tiny growls.

The biggest of the two finished and came to inspect me. I remained still as she poked around and nosed my leg. My lips twitched. I inched my hand out, and she sniffed my finger. The second kitten bounced over and bumped the first.

Soon, the kittens were crawling over my pants, up my shirt, and twining around my head. Little pricks of their claws registered on my skin, but I didn't care. It was like I'd gotten an experience that had been stolen from me in my childhood before I could realize what I was missing.

How could such a small body purr so loudly?

I cradled one in my hands. Both females.

Distantly, I heard Indy's car, but I didn't move, too entranced with creatures so tiny, I could close one in my fist.

"This isn't something I thought I'd ever see," Indy said in a low voice as she approached.

Looking up, I grinned. "They're cute."

Surprise flickered in her expression. "Kittens are known to be. Have you ever had one?"

I shook my head and held the kitten to my ear. "They're loud."

"Lachlan Jade, you've been enchanted." She dropped

next to me, and the kittens switched their attention to her. I couldn't be jealous. I was the same.

She wore a blue tank top and shorts. Scratches were healing on her legs, but she'd never wear pants in the summer, no matter what work she was doing. "Are we keeping them?"

"Can we?"

She whipped her head toward me. "Why are you asking?"

"I don't know. I've never had a pet. It seems like something that we should decide together."

"Mm." She picked up the kitten I'd been holding and held her nose to nose. The kitten's little whiskers twitched as she sniffed. "Outside or inside?"

"I... don't know."

She smiled. "I think you need the full experience, and that happens with indoor cats. The next strays that show up can be outdoor cats and help with the rodents. What should we name them?"

A name popped into my head from when I'd first seen them stalking the birdbath. "She's Birdie." The larger kitten had taken the lead hunting the bird. "And she's..."

"Eleven."

I gave Indy an inquisitive look.

She tapped her empty left wrist. "It's the time."

"Birdie and Eleven?" I liked them. I picked Eleven up, and she immediately started purring again.

"You're sweet with them." There was a hitch in her voice.

I cradled the kitten close to my chest. "Is everything okay?"

She nuzzled Birdie. "Seeing you with them made me

wonder about…" She ran her teeth over her lower lip. "A family."

Stunned, I couldn't reply. A family. Kids. I had hoped we'd reach that point, but I didn't think it would be this quickly. Unless she was telling me she didn't want to have kids with me.

"I thought—I mean, it was clear after we mated it wasn't something you were thinking about."

"I knew we weren't ready." Like she had. "And now?"

She tilted her head, and the kitten batted at her hair. "And now I'd like to see you with kids."

"Do you want kids?"

"Yes." Her smile was sweet. "Maybe not six."

"No." I barked a laugh. "I don't know what I'd do with a litter."

She giggled. "At least two. Maybe three. I like seeing how close you are with Venus and Ronan."

My mouth had suddenly gone dry. "When?"

"Let's give ourselves this year, and then we'll see what nature gives us."

Daily birth control worked on shifters. Our bodies could circumvent implants and shots. But a daily pill worked, and when Indy was ready, all she had to do was stop taking it.

My mind whirled like a county fair ride. Kids. Was practicing on kittens a good start? "Do we need stuff for Birdie and Eleven?"

"Litter boxes." She put Birdie down and smiled as the kitten stalked through the grass, her short little tail pointed in the air. "Food. They should see the vet. I'd guess they're a couple of months old, but Dr. Olson would know better."

The kittens weren't kids, but my family was growing. "Maybe we should invite your parents over for supper."

"First, I find you playing with kittens, and now you're inviting people to the house? What happened while I was gone?" Her tone was light, but I had to agree with her. This wasn't me.

It's who I wanted to be. "They're family, and I don't want to fall out of your mom's good graces and miss out on my blanket."

She laughed and rose, snatching Birdie up as the kitten was stalking a bug. "I'll call them. I have some ideas to run past both of you anyway."

~

INDY

MOM AND DAD wandered over the property I was showing them. It wouldn't be my first choice to build a cabin or two, but I didn't have many selections around Mirror Lake.

"This has had two offers fall through." I called the real estate agent, who was an old classmate, and pretended to be nosy. I didn't want her to know I was a prospective buyer. Not yet. Not until I talked to Penn. The Crockers motel had gotten everyone's hopes up. "Both times due to financing. No issues were found with the property."

Mom wandered by, working her chin between her thumb and forefinger. "It would work. Only a quarter mile from the road." This place was closer to the road and less private for shifters wanting to get away. "It's a farther walk to the trail, but it'd be a nice trek in the winter."

Outdoor activities appealed to our kind. Cross-country skiing and snowshoeing were as popular as ice fishing. "I think it'll be a popular spot. It's actually big enough for two cabins."

Dad had been spinning like a top losing its momentum. He pointed at one corner of the twenty-acre property. "There." He pivoted in the opposite direction. "And on the other side of the trees—there."

Two cabins here plus theirs was a good start, but it was hard to keep my mind on the property. I thought of my conversation with Lachlan over the kittens who'd been banished from the bedroom once Lachlan had gotten an ass full of claws.

I'd never forget how he so carefully cradled them to his chest as he took them to the hallway, talking gently but sternly to them, before returning to bed to finish devouring me.

Kids. I wanted to be a mother. I liked caring for those I loved. Was it because I wanted to care for a family of my own? I had a part-time job that'd give me a reprieve. The cabins would be like my crocheting projects. Mom used to leave the six of us with Dad while she packed her yarn and went on an overnight trip with her sister to craft.

Giddiness rose inside me, but I didn't want anyone to know until I was actually expecting. Enough people had opinions about my relationship.

"I think it's a fine choice." Mom grabbed Dad's hand. "Was that Beth that you talked to?"

"Yes, but I have to talk to Penn first. If he has ideas, then I'll give you the go-ahead to talk to her. Maybe there's other land for sale."

"You did good. If nothing else comes available, we can make this work." She gave me a hug, same with Dad, before they loaded up in their car and left.

I headed down the trail that connected this place to my parents' cabin. Using these wouldn't pose an issue with local wildlife. They were accustomed to us. Our scents were different than humans'. The animals that used these trails were more active during the day and wary of us when we shifted, which was more often after dark.

A urine scent slapped me in the face. I was yanking my tank top off before I registered the same stench smell from before. This was fresh. One or both were close by.

I toed out of my athletic shoes as I pushed down my shorts.

A growl reached my ears as I shifted.

Shit. I hadn't been lost in my head, but I also wasn't expecting to be stalked by another creature who thought themselves a predator.

Leaves rustled around me. My body elongated, but as my skin was changing to scales, claws raked down my side. My yell came out as half a roar. I gritted through the shift, maintaining the concentration needed.

The woods went silent as the mountain lion shifter continued attacking me. I spun, whacking my tail against a few trees. Glittering eyes flashed as a second mountain lion shifter launched at me. I was more ready for it. The cat on my back couldn't get a good hold with my scales. He was an irritant more than anything.

I snatched the big cat out of the air, my talons sinking into its hide. The same screams I'd heard before blasted from it. It wiggled and struggled out of my grip, but I snapped my jaws and took a chunk out of its haunches. It floundered. The first mountain lion flung itself at my face, but I flipped my head and shook it off.

Then I bit the head off the mountain lion in my grip.

Warm blood filled my mouth. I wanted to gag, but my beast rejoiced at the flavor and the kill. The second lion screamed, rage and anguish in the sound. It leaped, bypassing my face to get onto my neck. His claws scraped against my scales as he scrambled to get on my back.

He was going for my eyes.

I squeezed my eyes shut and surged sideways, whacking myself against a tree. Branches snapped and the big cat skittered off my back and thumped to the ground. But it was fast, darting for my belly.

My scales were strong on the underside of my body but not impenetrable. I rolled to my side and used my hind legs to shove it away. The crunch of a tree trunk cracked before it toppled over me.

The shifter scored my belly, not breaking far under the surface of the weaker scales. I roared and grabbed it with all four limbs, not caring what I got a hold of, and ripped the cat apart.

I released my grip, and the pieces of the mountain lion flopped lifeless, morphing into his human form. A man.

A second body lay on the path. A woman, judging from the anatomy. I couldn't tell from the face I'd destroyed.

I shifted to my human form, stumbling backward as my hind legs turned into regular legs. Losing my balance, I thumped to my ass. The tree that had fallen on me arched over the trail and was held up by sturdy trees I hadn't battered down.

Turning, I heaved onto the ground. All my lunch came

up, and each time I sucked in a breath, I smelled blood and death. My body shook as I threw up until I didn't have anything left to give.

I took a few minutes to gather myself. Fighting to kill wasn't like training with my siblings. If I hadn't been so experienced getting jumped by my oldest brothers and sisters, I might've been gutted. But still, it was odd for mountain lions to take on a dragon.

I scrambled on my hands and knees to my scattered clothing. I wasn't getting dressed. It was hard not to shift back to my dragon just in case. With trembling hands, I found my phone and called Lachlan.

"Hey." His voice was warm, and I hated to intrude on his good mood.

"Lachlan. Something happened."

~

LACHLAN

I SQUATTED BY THE BODIES, furious I couldn't shred them. They'd wanted to attack Indy alone. Had they planned it, or had they seized the opportunity?

Levi crouched next to me. He'd returned from meeting with Deacon in Silver Lake for the last week. He'd called it his warm-up since the Silver clan leader was reasonable and held no resentments against Peridot. Their arrogance had earned them bitterness from the other clans.

"Think they were a couple?" he asked.

"Possible." I snapped a picture of the male. He was in

a few pieces. What had possessed him to take on a dragon shifter?

Blood had quit seeping through Indy's shirt as she healed. Superficial wounds that could've been worse. If they'd been able to gut her and get her on the ground, she could've been killed.

But my girl was a fighter.

Pride filled me as much as concern. Word would get out, and I wouldn't worry Indy's reputation suffered from her family's protective cocoon. She'd been attacked, and she'd come out the victor. But a part of her would be changed.

"That's gross," Levi said, watching me take pictures. It wasn't as if dragon shifter communities had a forensics team.

I didn't care to have pictures of corpses on my phone, but I had a job to do. "I'll have to show the Montgomery pack and see if they know them." And if they didn't, I'd work my way out from there.

"What about... her?"

The other attacker's ID would be challenging with no face and all. "Go and see if she has any identifying birthmarks."

Levi stared toward the remains of the other attacker. He didn't want to do what I asked. "Is it wrong to hope I don't find any so I don't have to take a picture?"

"Understandable."

He shook his head, and his boots crunched against the dirt on the path. I remained crouched, but my gaze settled on Indy's back. She'd dressed, but when we'd arrived, she'd been midshift, prepared to attack us, hyper-aware of the movement before she smelled our approach.

As if she sensed me, she glanced over her shoulder. Her gaze wasn't forlorn, to my relief. She wasn't getting lost in her head. A hardness surrounded her that hadn't been there before. A determination. She'd be okay. But killing someone was an act she'd have to live with, self-defense or not.

"Is there anything I can do?" she asked, her voice quiet.

I shook my head and rose. "No. I'll have to go to nearby packs and see if anyone can ID them."

Her mouth tightened. "Should I come with?"

"No. Then it'd be seen as personal. With just me, it becomes shifter politics. Two of theirs were camping and stalking my people."

"They'll believe that?"

I rubbed the back of my neck. Levi was using a branch to move the other shifter's remains, peering underneath like a snake was going to strike out. There were nothing but harmless snakes around here. "It'll depend on who they identify. If they want to start trouble, they'll get defensive, but since I've made good with Silver clan, I doubt they'll risk it."

She nodded and continued staring into the trees, her knees hugged to her chest.

"I'd like Levi to stay here while I'm gone," I said.

She twisted to look at me again, a slight frown on her face.

"It'll show clan unity between the dragon shifters," I explained. A valid excuse but not completely honest. "And I'd feel better if you were being specifically targeted."

I might have to visit a few packs. I could be led on a wild-goose chase, and Indy could be alone for weeks.

She finally nodded. "That's a good idea."

Levi wandered toward us. "Happy to help. You can leave some paperwork or whatever for me to do while you're gone." The guy liked having a purpose. He'd been willing to do whatever I asked as long as there was a point. He was a lot like Ronan that way.

I lifted my chin to the body he'd been searching. "Anything?"

"A strawberry kiss by her hip. That's what my mom used to call them. She said that was how she could tell Memphis and Maverick apart as babies."

I wouldn't need a picture. "I'll leave in the morning. You might as well come over for supper."

He gave me a lopsided grin meant to defuse some of the tension. "You cooking for me?"

"I'll throw something in the oven. The only thing I cook is sandwiches and tuna pouches." I held out a hand for Indy. She gripped it but didn't need my support to rise. I gave Levi my pickup keys. "I'll ride back with Indy."

Levi helped me pull the bodies to the side of the trail. The walk back to the cabin was quiet. We left the carnage behind. I wouldn't respect them after what they'd done. Their pack could retrieve them or leave them to the other predators.

Levi took off in my pickup as I loaded Indy up.

She let out a sigh and rolled her gaze toward me. "I want to go home and take a long shower."

"You clean up. I'll get something in the oven and work on the plans with Levi."

"Thank you."

"For what?"

"For not treating me with kid gloves. I'm still stunned, but I'll get over it."

Getting over it was the wrong way to look at what happened. "You never forget it."

She shuddered. "Yeah. I don't think I could."

I wouldn't either. Whoever was behind this was going to pay.

CHAPTER

ELEVEN

L achlan

THE SECOND PACK I went to was an hour away from Jade Hills, and the third pack I'd visited in as many days. I'd gone home between each visit so whoever was behind this didn't think I was out of town for days.

The second day had soured my mood when it came to this already aggravating task. I'd visited another pack, and the leader had avoided me, making me think he was hiding something, only for me to find him sloppy drunk with two females. Neither was his mate, and he hadn't wanted to be found.

The current pack I was meeting with was just across the border and conveniently called the Border pack. I hated crossing into Canada. I didn't have time for questions when I wasn't up to shit.

What are you going to Canada for?

Then the stern glare. It had to be a shit job when you didn't know who was smuggling, trafficking, up to no good, and who just wanted to see a different country. I could smell a strong lie, but the humans at the Port of Entry had to use a mixture of gut instinct and mind-numbing routine.

Shifters could become border patrol agents, but most didn't want to figure out how to circumvent the *Because I can smell the drugs better than the dogs* intuition. There was such a thing as being too good at a job.

I pulled into the small town across the border. Trees surrounded me on all sides. The place was barely on the map and mixed with humans and mountain lion shifters. Even a few wolf shifters had settled in the community.

I went straight to a square red farmhouse a few blocks off Main Street, which meant it was almost out of town.

The door opened as soon as I climbed out. An older woman with almost black hair streaked with gray wandered onto the wide porch. I had based the porch on my house off it. Big enough for a rocking chair, or several smaller chairs for company. Part of me had felt delusional. Company?

But when Indy's parents had come over the other night, we'd sat out there. Indy had lit citronella candles, and most of the mosquitoes had been dissuaded. I hadn't been able to believe it. Me. My house. Entertaining.

"Enid," I said with a tilt of my head. She was the undisputed leader of the pack. Several young males had tried to overthrow her, thinking her age made her weak instead of cunning and experienced. They'd been wrong.

"Lachlan Jade. I've heard there's trouble."

She'd been notified by the other pack leader I'd talked to. There were no hard feelings. I'd do no less. "I need to show you a couple of photos. They're gruesome."

"I doubt I need to see the pictures. I can guess who it is."

Interested, I crested the stairs. She waved to a seat, and I accepted, knowing she might not share any information with me. Clan politics could be tricky among the shifters. Dragons had their pride. Mountain lions could get a little salty, too cunning for their own good. Wolves could either take the pack idea or the one-wolf idea too seriously. And bears were touch and go. Bear shifters didn't hibernate, but that didn't mean I was willing to pester them during the winter months.

I handed Enid my phone, unconcerned she'd scroll through the rest. The only pictures I had were for work. Studying her reaction, I had my answer almost immediately.

She smacked her lips against her teeth. "Yeah, they're ours."

"Feral?"

She snorted and slowly rocked her chair. "I wish I could use that as an excuse. No, they fancied themselves rebels. Smarter than me. They kept pushing their limits until one time last year, I challenged them both, but they slunk away in the middle of the night."

"Any idea why they'd be camping in Jade Hills?" By the remains of where I'd grown up? The place was abandoned, but there was enough movement in and around the area surrounding the lake, I had thought squatters would be deterred. I'd been wrong.

"You're better to answer that than me."

I frowned. "What do you mean?"

"They were all buddy-buddy with a dragon shifter. Craig—that's the male's name—let it slip at the bar. The male was a Jade."

Dread crawled over my skin. There was a plot within my clan? Against me? Indy? "Did he give a name?"

She shook her head. "That'd be too easy, Lachlan." She adopted a sly smile. "But I followed them. They never noticed me."

I had to root myself into my seat or I would've scooted to the end. Never look too eager for information.

She didn't continue. Shit. She wanted something in return. "How much is this information worth?"

Her eyes glittered. "You never were brainless like your parents." Her chair squeaked as she rocked. "I have a granddaughter. She doesn't fit in here."

"How old?"

"Twenty-three."

"I'm mated."

She nodded in time with the rock of her chair. "You are. But that Peridot you've got sniffing around the other dragon shifter clans isn't."

What the hell? I'd been in on the plan to send Ronan to Garnet River, but I wasn't a fucking matchmaker. "What exactly do you want?"

"You know what it's like when your family leaves a legacy, good or bad." It wasn't a question, but when I dipped my head, she continued. "It's the opposite for Briony. She's a gentle soul."

Ah, hell. "And that personality doesn't do well in the shifter world."

"But Deacon's mate is human, and from what I hear,

very much like Briony. The Garnet ruler had to prove herself, but the clan tolerated her when they didn't know she could handle herself. Briony won't get the same treatment here. She's returned from college, and males are already sniffing around her, thinking of challenging her for the right to mate her."

I hid my distaste for the mountain lion shifter's age-old but rarely used custom for *might made right* when it came to mating. Ironic, coming from me. But if Indy had balked, I wouldn't have forced her. I definitely wouldn't have fought her for the right to mount her. It wouldn't be so bad, but if a male, or female, was willing to kick the shit out of the person they wanted to mate, the relationship had an astronomical chance of being abusive. Clearly, Enid felt the same or she wouldn't be trying to arrange a mating for her granddaughter with a shifter no mountain lion would challenge.

"I'm not Levi Peridot's ruler. Have you talked to his sister?"

The steady squeak answered for her, but she still said, "No, but I'd like to know if it's true—his council wants him mated."

I gave her an even look. I wouldn't comment on other clan's business.

She stared into the street. "Too bad. Have a good trip back to your country."

I wasn't compromising my position. I could get the information another way. "Thanks for talking with me."

As I rose, the front door banged open. A curvy girl with golden-brown hair stomped out. "Grandma, you can't mate me off."

Enid's expression was stern. "I can and I will."

Briony rounded on me. "I don't know if the Jade I saw in town was the same one talking to Craig, but he was a well-dressed male with dark hair." She waved her fingers over her forehead. "Trendy style."

"Briony, dammit," Enid snapped. "Don't interfere."

Briony only wrinkled her pert little nose. She might be a gentle soul, but she was ornery.

I didn't have a picture of Dallas, but the description fit. "I appreciate it." I looked to Enid. "I'll talk to Levi."

"No," Briony said.

"Levi's a good guy." I didn't like to dabble in other clan's business, but Enid would destroy herself protecting Briony, and my life was easier with Enid as a pack leader. "I'll talk to Memphis, but you should give her a call. There's no harm in talking." There was, but it could also be good if the males in Border pack thought Briony was getting paired off with a dragon shifter.

"Hmph," the females said at the same time.

I tipped my head.

"Wait," Briony said. "I overheard Cheryl mention a woman when I was out for a walk. She was arguing with Craig in the grocery store parking lot."

"Does Cheryl have a strawberry birthmark near her hip?" I asked.

Briony nodded. "It's a—was a running joke about how many males had kissed the target." So Craig and Cheryl were my attackers. "I heard her yelling at Craig. She said that bitch had better pay or they'd walk. Craig wanted to settle, but Cheryl was greedy."

Enid nodded. "She was like that."

Was it possible I wasn't chasing Dallas? "Thanks. Do you want to retrieve the bodies?"

Enid smacked her lips again. "Let the birds peck their

bones dry. It's more than they deserve if they hunted your mate."

I walked back to my pickup, planning to call Memphis and put in my two cents about Briony when I returned to Jade Hills. Enid's last comment proved why I needed her to stay in power instead of losing her for a stubborn granddaughter.

~

INDY

LACHLAN WOULDN'T BE BACK until later. I worked at the cabin, seeing the place with new eyes. I walked through the back of the house. I could build a patio with a firepit. That'd be a draw for a rental.

A picnic table and... I didn't know, but I wanted to ask Lachlan if we could go to Lake Metigoshe one weekend to see what they offered with their cabins. My parents had gone there a few times when I was little. I remembered the picnic table and firepits. Horseshoe poles. But the lake was meant for water activities. Mirror Lake that this cabin was close to was meant for fishing. Would anyone be interested?

I wasn't talking myself out of this. I could make it work. We didn't need a party lake. People wanted a getaway where they could be their shifter selves and this would serve all sorts of shifters.

Prickles rose along my skin. Someone was approaching. Had Lachlan returned early? He'd just messaged me to say he was leaving Border pack.

I rounded the cabin and pulled up short. Dallas

wandered out from the trees, wearing gray sweats and athletic shoes with no shirt.

He spotted me but didn't smile. "Indy. We need to talk."

I willed my pulse to remain as close to normal as possible. "Why?"

He jerked his head toward the trail he'd just come from. "I have something to show you."

I held up a hand. "I was just attacked. I'm not going anywhere with you." He took a step forward, but I shoved my arm out farther. "Stop." My brain was calculating how quickly I could shed my clothing.

Two mountain lion shifters were different than a full-grown male dragon shifter.

"I don't want to hurt you."

"Is that what you told Lily?" Shit, I shouldn't have gone there. I was in enough danger as it was. Had Dallas sent those shifters after me? And why?

Confusion twisted his features. "Lily? What does she have to do with us?"

I dropped my arm and lifted my chin. I had opened the door. It was time to go through. "I don't want to disappear like her."

"I didn't do anything to her," he said tightly. He shook his head like he was dislodging a swarm of bees. "Lily has nothing to do with us. You refuse to see Lachlan for what he is."

"And what is that?"

"A liar."

I barked out a laugh. "Oh, really?"

Agitated, Dallas jerked a finger down the path he'd come from, the one that ran between the cabin and Lachlan's parents' place. "If you would just come and see. I'll explain everything."

"How about no?"

He lifted his chin and his desperation diminished, replaced with determination. "Lachlan killed his parents."

The certainty he spoke with kept me from scoffing. Everyone knew what had happened to Lachlan's parents. "Why do you think that?"

"I'm not the only one who thinks so. The evidence is there. They were killed before the fire broke out."

"Since when are you an expert in forensics?"

"We dug them up."

The oily feeling snaked through my organs. "We?"

"Look." He stabbed a hand through his hair. His abs rippled. His body had been the excuse I used to tell myself that dating him was just fine. That I was feeling off because I was so inexperienced. "I-I ran into those shifters, and they were telling me that nothing about that place makes sense."

"You were working with the mountain lion shifters?" And I was at the cabin. Alone. I had speculated Dallas was a killer, but reality settled on my shoulders like a ton of rocks.

"No. I said I *talked* to them. I asked what they were doing snooping around the woods."

Was he lying? His eyes said he believed what he said, but his agitation made me think there was a lie buried here, and it wasn't Lachlan's. "How would they know?"

"The way the house was searched. They knew exactly where the bodies were. It was the middle of the night. Shouldn't they have been in the bedroom?"

I had thought the same. Unease made me back up a step. "It doesn't mean anything."

"The glass in the windowpane is gone, but the pane itself is open. They could've escaped. They wouldn't have passed out from the smoke."

I knew nothing about fires. "Wouldn't the oxygen fuel the flames?"

"Things are broken. All over the living room. If you look through what survived, it's all there. The old couch had molded away, but the frame is busted. There's a hole in the wall."

"Maybe they tried to bust their way outside."

"They could've used the door."

Well, that made sense. "What do you want me to think?"

"That Lachlan didn't earn his position. He killed his parents and lied about it, and he's been ruling under false pretenses. And he got you with those lies."

I hadn't been attracted to Lachlan because of his position. His quiet strength was a direct line to my libido. "And why would he do that?"

"I don't know. But if I'm right, and he hasn't told you, then you might want to ask yourself what that means."

Lachlan's earlier words streamed through my brain. He wasn't ready to tell me everything, and he wasn't sure he'd ever be. I wondered what kind of secret would satisfy all the factors—it didn't involve me but would threaten everything else. It could blow back on his family and change what everyone thought of him.

Killing his parents without issuing a fair challenge would do it.

I didn't reply, and Dallas's gaze grew more intense. "Next time you're there, take a look around. The rubble was moved to the side, not out. Lachlan knew exactly where to find his parents' bodies."

He surprised me by turning to walk back the way he'd come. He'd said his piece, and he was done.

This didn't make sense. None of it made sense. Dallas hadn't tried to kill me. He'd been worried, fervent. He'd mentioned the mountain lion shifters like he had nothing to hide. He'd wanted to warn me. Like I'd been tricked into my mating, and he didn't want that for me.

The so-called evidence he'd brought up was weak. But still... what if?

I took one last look at the cabin, and for a moment, I was tempted to go to the rubble of the elder Jades' place and have another look. Dallas might still be there, and in the end, searching wouldn't give me the answer I needed. Only Lachlan could do that.

I drove home and made myself a sandwich, munching on it as the kittens played at my feet. They tumbled across the floor, keeping me from sinking into my thoughts so far I didn't notice the time.

Just as I looked at my phone and thought Lachlan should be rolling in, he pulled into the garage. I stayed where I was, brushing the crumbs off my shirt and fingers.

I was asking my husband for complete honesty, and I didn't want to look like a hot mess.

He came into the house and entered the kitchen, his mellow expression filling with concern when his gaze landed on me. He crossed to me, giving me a quick kiss on the forehead, then stood back. "What's wrong?"

The kitchen had to be full of my emotion. Angst. Consternation. If Dallas was on to something—even more, if he was right—then what?

"I talked to Dallas." When his gaze darkened, I shook my head. "He didn't try to do anything but tell me something."

He folded his arms across his chest and leaned against the island. "Okay."

I took a deep breath. "He said he thinks you killed your parents and lied about the fire."

TWELVE

L achlan

My worst nightmare had just come true. I could save the fantasy I had built. I could lie. But Indy would always wonder. She'd suspect. We were growing too close for her to believe a blatant lie.

"It's true." I hoped the truth would be a relief if it ever came out, but the shame was staggering. "It's all true," I said hoarsely.

She didn't look at me like I was revolting. Only with measured disbelief. "You killed them?"

"I had to." I let my head drop back. The story poured out. "Our council had arranged the mating between Venus and Deacon."

She nodded. Everyone had known Venus was contracted to the Silver ruler, but she'd taken her time.

Same with him, until he'd met Ava and wanted her instead—to Venus's great relief, and Penn's.

"You fought with them over Venus?"

"It was the tipping point. They had this get-rich-quick scheme. They were going to sell her."

Indy recoiled, horror in her eyes. "They'd incur the father of Silver clan for money?"

"Not if it looks like Venus took another mate. Not if it was another shifter. The deal would be secret. I just happened to overhear them."

"And then what?"

"And then..." I let out a heavy exhale. "I told them they wouldn't do that. I'd challenged Mom and then Dad got pissed because of that and because he hated being reminded that he wasn't the one who'd been born to rule."

"That's when you fought?"

I nodded. "I don't remember much. I just blanked and didn't stop until they weren't moving. And then I took Dad's lighter and..." I lifted a shoulder. The rest wasn't history. It haunted me every day. "I wanted nothing of them and their legacy of pain and death left." I let out a sigh. That part had been a deliberate decision. I owned what I had done, but that didn't mean I wouldn't do it differently all over again. "When the town thought they both died in the fire, I let them. It was easier. I'd be challenged, and I'd win, and the town would be divided because of it."

Sympathy filled her gaze. "The family of whoever you challenged would turn against you."

I wouldn't have been challenged by people like Dallas. Guys whose parents weren't in the town's good graces. I'd have been challenged by those who'd been encouraged to take on my parents because the town trusted them.

"You killed them for your sister, and you lied about it for the town." She stepped closer to me. I didn't move. I didn't deserve it. "And you thought I wouldn't love you anymore."

"I didn't think you'd ever love me. Once I had it, I wasn't losing it."

She nodded, her dark eyes shining. "I love you, Lachlan. And I don't know where we'll go from here now that Dallas suspects the truth, but nothing changes between us. I'd want to be with you anyway."

I gripped her around her hips and spun to set her ass on the counter. "Be sure of what you say. I could be driven out. I could be challenged."

She settled her hands on my shoulders but didn't try to get out of my grasp. "You would win."

I would. My parents had ensured it. "Aren't you disgusted by me?" Our kind didn't tolerate lies and deceit, and it was a death knell for a position of power.

"No. I'm proud of you." She placed a kiss on my lips. "I'm glad you told me." Another kiss. "And I understand why you kept it a secret."

"Now what?" I asked, leaning my forehead against hers.

"Now, you make love to me."

The way she said it, I almost believed she really loved me. But I knew how I felt. "I've been in love with you for years."

Her smile was sweet before she captured my mouth. I didn't let her go after that. She wanted to make love, and before now, I would've thought that meant long, slow sex, filled with lingering touches and gazes full of the love in our hearts.

But in this moment, it was getting inside my mate as soon as possible. It was connecting with her so with each thrust, she could know that she was everything. It would be the cherry on top of our relationship.

I wouldn't only show her I loved her in bed. If that meant taking her on the kitchen island, then I was dropping my fucking pants.

I wrenched my fly open, and Indy wiggled out of her shorts. I helped her get them down her legs and off until they were on the floor. We hadn't broken our kiss.

I hesitated only to make sure my mate was ready before shoving inside. A mixed groan and whimper left her. I was surrounded by heaven, and I kept thrusting. A needy moan went from her mouth to mine. I grunted and thrust again.

This female knew everything about me, and she still loved me. The question of whether I'd done the right thing faded to nothing. I had chosen her for a reason. She had captured my attention because she was meant to be mine.

When my orgasm hit, I held her closer. She did the same. We'd never been more connected.

Trembles ran through my body. I'd never shaken like this before. I released her mouth. Her eyelids were heavy, and we were only a breath apart, still connected otherwise.

"I'll never quit loving you," I said. "No matter what happens."

She kissed the corner of my mouth. "We stay together."

"I want to take you to bed." I wanted to spend the

whole night buried inside of her. I wanted to love her until morning. Yet, with the revelation, there were things I needed to do.

"You have to call Venus and Ronan."

I touched our foreheads together again. "Yes. After you, they should be the next to know. Dallas thought telling you would drive you farther away."

"It didn't work," she whispered.

"Because you're amazing." I nuzzled her neck and my cock twitched inside of her. "But he's going to up his game. I need to be ready."

With that, my dick fully deflated. I helped her down.

She grabbed her shorts, her round ass sticking in the air. Couldn't my tasks wait?

No.

She straightened and caught me staring. She bit her lower lip, appearing to struggle with parting as much as I was. "I'll jump in the shower. When you're done, come to bed."

"As soon as I can."

I watched her ass sway as she left the room. Sensing we were done fornicating, the kittens rushed back in and twined around my legs. I gave them a few scratches behind the ears before I palmed my phone and went outside. Dropping on the front stoop, I dialed Venus. I was never one to shy away from the hard stuff, and I was done living in fear of the one time I had.

"AND THIS ENID wants me to mate her?" Levi asked. He was sprawled in the chair across from my desk. He was wearing basketball shorts and no shirt. Before he came into my office, he'd shoved his feet into flip-flops.

He might look like he just rolled out of bed, but I'd caught him when he'd finished in the gym. I doubted the Peridot council looked too deep at Levi. On the surface, his looks and his cavalier smile made him seem like he didn't take anything seriously. Just because he didn't walk around with a murderous expression like me didn't mean he wasn't serious.

"Yes. Briony is a few years younger than you. She'd know what she's getting into."

His face screwed up. "No shifter other than a dragon has been mated into Peridot for ages. And you think it'll help me if I do it?"

I inclined my head. "I don't think it'll hurt as much as you think. Memphis mentioned the close calls with people from your clan." With the lack of dating options, people were waiting to mate until they were at risk of termination. The unions weren't happy, and if they were on paper only, then they weren't productive. Too many more generations and Peridot would fade out of existence.

Clans couldn't be allowed to isolate themselves. If a dragon shifter married any other shifter, the child would be a dragon shifter. Same with a human mate. It was a way to keep our population from diminishing.

"If Memphis did it, maybe. Maverick. But me?" He shook his head, running a hand across the front of his brow, shuffling his hair to the side. It looked like he spent hundreds at Venus's salon instead of doing a hard work-out. "They'll make life hell for her. If she can't stand up to her pack, she won't survive mine."

"I don't know." At his quizzical look, I explained. "I

don't know if she *can't* stand up to her pack. She won't. She was raised entitled, and despite Enid's best intentions, she protected her granddaughter."

"So you're trying to set me up with a spoiled girl who doesn't care how her attitude affects the people who run the pack?"

That was... Shit. Was I? I thought of Briony and her compact curves and short stature. "I think it's more than that. Not quite false bravado, but an insecurity she's hiding. Maybe she has an out. All I could tell was Enid would fight to the death for her, and she'll be a target if anything happens. The Border pack is closer allies than any other. Enid's always taken care of business, and her son will do the same. But her daughter died and left Briony behind and..."

"She's their weak link. And I'm her immunity."

"Exactly."

He rested his chin in his fingers. "And you haven't talked to Memphis?"

"I wanted you to be informed."

He thought for a moment. "I haven't even met her."

"Are you open to it?"

He wrinkled his nose. "God, no."

Damn. My hopes tanked.

He ran his hands over his face. "But, hell. I haven't even hit a third date since high school. It's been a hookup or a fizzle. Or both." He ruffled his hair again, and again, it fell artfully in place. Briony had to be attracted to him. Or was that too easy? "I'll call Memphis. I'll tell her, but I think I should finish visiting the clans first."

"Good idea." If the clans thought he favored the pack over them, they'd take it out on relations with Peridot.

"So… gonna tell me what you were extra growly about this morning?"

I hadn't been worse than normal. I'd called Venus and Ronan. Venus had sworn up a storm, then told me she and Penn would leave Garnet River immediately. I told her not to come back early for me. I needed to face this on my own.

Then she'd thanked me.

Ronan had done the same, and they both said that if they had been in my position, they would've done what I had. From the fight to the lie. Their validation was a huge hurdle, but the ultimate judgment would be up to the clan.

I'd have to tell the council. Then we'd come up with a plan to tell the town.

"It's a work in progress," I answered.

Disappointment crossed his face. We'd been working together since he'd arrived, and now I left him hanging. "There are people who need to know first. People who are owed the explanation before you. Kind of like having to visit the clans first."

"Got it."

I checked the time on my computer screen. "Hey, I gotta meet Indy."

"No worries. Now that I've sweated all over your office chair, I should shower."

"Send the chair to Briony and let her get used to your musk."

Levi's laugh sputtered out of him as he stood. "Sometimes I forget you have a sense of humor. I like to surprise females with my musk, thank you very much."

My humor faded as he walked out. I could pretend

today was a normal day, but I had started the day emailing the council for a meeting.

Tomorrow at one. It was business as usual until then.

I grabbed a stack of papers on the edge of my desk. Then I locked my office and left the armory. I was meeting Indy at Griffin's again. The restaurant was quickly becoming our spot, but lunch today wasn't exactly personal.

When I reached the restaurant, Porter was working again. He swallowed hard when he saw me. "Mr. Lachlan, sir. Jade. Mr. Jade."

"Ah, Lachlan is fine. Is Indy here yet?"

"Follow me." He led me to the same area they seemed to like putting us in.

Indy was poring over the menu, but she sensed me and looked up. Catching my eye, she grinned. "Hey. Thanks, Porter."

He ducked his head and opened his mouth, then snapped it shut.

"Go ahead." I liked Porter. He was going to be a good shifter to have in the clan if he stayed in Jade Hills after he was done with school. He was respectful of leadership, but there was a sense of strength surrounding him.

He glanced around. "Can I talk to you later? In your office or something?"

Surprised, I said, "Stop by anytime." Hopefully, it was after tomorrow's meeting.

He ducked his head and rushed away.

"I wonder what that was about," Indy murmured.

I didn't know, but I wasn't going to force him to tell me. "He'll tell me in his own time."

The server came by and we ordered right away. Once she left, I flourished the documents I'd brought.

Her gaze dropped to the papers I set on the table. "You said this was a work lunch. And it includes me?"

I spread each sheet out. On them were various plot maps. "This is the land we own."

Her eyes flared as she glanced at each sheet. "I knew you owned land but not this much."

"My parents were ruthless. And it's not mine. It's ours." Even after the truth got out, I would fight for what was mine. Because it was ours and Indy had a long-term goal in mind. She had the welfare of the town in mind, and that was my priority all along. "I thought you could see if any of the properties could work into the cabin rental plans."

"Lachlan, that's just…"

"I mean it." I tapped one of the sheets. "This is ours." I pointed to the next plot map. "This is adjacent to what's left of my parents' place. You could rebuild."

"Would that bother you?"

"It almost makes me laugh to think of their ending being a morbid attraction for others. Maybe some of the people they terrorized would find some sort of closure."

Her smile was soft, understanding. "Are you thinking in addition to the property my parents were looking at?"

"I think you decide how many rentals. I don't want to suck up extra property and leave nothing for people to buy."

"Right, I was wondering about that. The rentals could draw people to town, but if they find love and want to stay, I'd—" Her gaze shot to mine. "What if we developed?"

"You want to build?"

She nodded, excitement dancing in her eyes. I helped put that there. "Mom and Dad could buy the first place we looked at. It'd fit family homes better. And if Jade Hills is visibly growing?" She leaned back in the booth. "You'd have turned this town around in less than one generation."

"Do it."

She peered at the papers again. "I think four cabins would be sufficient. My parents' place. Your parents' old place and then"—she slid her finger to another sheet—"here. Spaced out. They're not on top of the town, and they have the lake and trails for recreation."

"We'll get the permits through the council. They're going through your outdated laws."

She sobered. "You talk to them tomorrow?"

"That's the meeting." My future wasn't unstable, but I didn't want to have to fight for it. There'd been enough bloodshed.

I gathered the papers when the food arrived. We'd bring the details to the council. I didn't need rumors getting out before then.

After we finished, I walked out with her. The sun was high overhead, like a promise that everything would be alright.

She'd parked across the street. I handed her the papers. She shuffled through them and squinted at me. "I really appreciate this, that we're doing this together and that you support me."

"Always." I gave her a kiss.

The hair rose on the back of my neck. I pulled away, and she was giving me a little smile when it faltered.

She looked over my shoulder, and her eyes widened. "Dallas?"

I turned, keeping her behind me. The rage rolling off

him hit me from where he was standing in the middle of the street.

"You don't believe me!" he roared to Indy.

Porter jogged out of Griffin's and stopped outside the door. Shit. This was going to attract a crowd.

"Dallas," Indy said in a calm tone. "I listened to you, and that's what you wanted. Lachlan and I have talked."

He drew himself up. "So I was right."

Another couple darted out of Griffin's and watched next to Porter. Others came out of the drugstore and the bank next to it. Dallas must've marched out of one of the buildings when he saw us.

"It'll all come out, Dallas," I said, unsure of how to handle this. The council should know first.

"You killed your parents and lied!" he yelled and ripped his polo shirt in two. Tossing the scraps aside, he bellowed, "I challenge you!"

"Damn," Indy said behind me.

"It's not your fault," I reassured her. "It's all mine."

By now, more people were lining the street. I took my shirt off and set it on the trunk of Indy's car.

Dallas pointed at me, red blotching his chest and face. He was naked already. "Our leader lied about earning his position. He killed his parents in cold blood and took the seat."

I finished stripping, unashamed of my nudity. "It's true." I strode toward him, my voice lifted. "They were awful, and I'd had enough. I'd had enough of death and force, and I didn't tell anyone what happened. I let you all assume."

Gazes burned into my skin.

Dallas's face twisted. "You should've been challenged years ago."

"I would've won." I had believed it then. I believe it now. "You don't have to do this."

"I don't want a pass." Spittle flew out of his mouth. "I. Challenge. You. Like someone should've been able to do then."

He was right, but it was going to end the same. "Jade has had enough death."

Dallas flung his arms out and spun around. "Behold your coward of a leader. He won't be in charge much longer." He settled his gaze on Indy. "And then you'll be mine."

"I'll never be yours, Dallas," she said.

A snarl ripped out of him before he shifted.

I turned into my dragon, relishing the power flooding my veins. The only highlight of the moment. Only one of us would make it out of this fight, and there would be destruction. I'd try to keep the buildings intact, but the cars on the street would suffer. We couldn't take this battle in the air, not in broad daylight.

As soon as the thought passed through my mind, Dallas launched himself, spreading his wings like he was going to take flight. I slammed forward, snagging him by a leg with my mouth, and jerked him down. He was off-kilter, and I body-slammed him to the pavement.

I could've ended him there. The guy was an inexperienced fighter, but I backed off to give him a chance. Letting out a roar, I circled him on the ground. A message to keep his feet on the pavement.

He didn't try to take flight again, but he fluttered his wings as if to psych me out. Steadying himself, he faced me. His dull green dragon was smaller than mine, and his scales lacked the jade sheen mine did. I was born into the ruling family. I had special skills that gave me an advantage, like extra healing and breathing fire.

I wouldn't use them.

My mind spun. I hated to kill Dallas in front of the town, but he'd challenged me. If I let him, he'd only return, more intent than before. There had to be a way. I hated to kill one of my clan because he was nothing more than an arrogant idiot.

If I knew he was behind Lily's death, it would be different. This would be justice, but I didn't know.

He lunged, intending to fake me out again, but I went for him. I got my teeth around his neck and flipped him to the side.

A rage-filled roar spilled from his mouth, but he righted himself and came after me again. I tucked my wings and body-slammed into him. We tumbled, and I dug my claws into his sides, wedging under the scales, anchoring myself so I could control the landing.

We stopped with me on top, both of us butted against a Ford Taurus, the bumper dented. He snapped at me with his powerful jaws and I headbutted him. A crack resounded through town, and murmurs traveled through the onlookers.

Indy was watching all of this, but I couldn't afford to be distracted by her.

Dallas flung me off. I let him. Would he give up when he saw he was outmatched?

He righted himself and let out another bellow. I paced, my tail dragging on the ground so the barbed tips could scrape against the cement. A menacing sound. My parents had been so adept at creating fear because they used mental tactics as well as physical. They fought dirty, and it was the small things that used to win their battles.

Dallas staggered as he tried to face me. His mouth was open in a way that would've been a sneer had he been in his human form. His eyes were wild and his breathing erratic.

He knew.

He knew this fight wasn't his to win. He knew he fucked up. And he knew that he'd die.

I willed him to appeal to my humanity. I'd let him live unless I could prove he killed his ex-girlfriend. And then I'd feel justified with his execution.

But this time, when he lunged, he bypassed me.

Indy.

She was on the sidewalk where I left her.

Her gasp reached me, fueling my determination. Dallas was fast, I'd give him that. She was backing up to press herself against the building, but his jaw was open, and she was small enough to fit right inside.

I latched my teeth around his tail and yanked. His feet slipped out from under him and his jaws clacked together when his snout hit the pavement. I dragged him away from my mate, back into the middle of the street.

Dallas had to die.

It wasn't fun. It wasn't satisfying. I flung him around until I could anchor him to the pavement and close my jaw around his neck. His answering roar cut off into a scream.

Decapitating dragons wasn't easy. We weren't like wolf shifters or mountain lion shifters. Bears were even much easier. Dragons had scales, and one bite wasn't enough. But Dallas never had a chance to recover. I severed the last of his flesh, and his body went limp under me.

I didn't stagger back. I gathered myself before

pushing off him. Then I stepped aside, using my wings for balance. Adrenaline made me want to surge into the air and barrel roll just to burn off the excess.

I stayed on the ground, swallowing the drive to rage through the town and make everyone pay for what Dallas did. His human form was limp in the street, as gruesome as the shifters Indy had killed.

Changing back to my human form, I wished I could clean the blood off me before speaking to the people lining the street.

There would be no chance. I kept my voice steady. "Dallas has lost the challenge. Anyone else?"

I met the stares of the people around me. Shock was the most common expression. They were stunned they'd gone from a normal workday to a battle in the streets. It hadn't happened for years. Not since I took the role of ruler.

I kept my voice raised so I was clear. "I will discuss it today with my council. We'll have a town meeting so you can be fully informed about what happened should anyone want to challenge me." I spun in a slow circle, nude and full of blood. Not everyone in the town had heard Dallas or witnessed the fight, but news would travel fast. "I did what I thought was best for this clan. And I'd do it again."

I gave a nod before crossing to Indy. Would she shrink away? Would the gore remind her of her fight?

But she closed the distance between us and reached her hand out. I closed mine around it and grabbed my clothing from the back of the car. Without dressing, I got into the passenger seat.

Indy slid behind the wheel. "Let's go home."

THIRTEEN

$\mathcal{I}$ ndy

LEVI SLID into the seat next to me in the old armory's auditorium. It was only yesterday that Lachlan had terminated Dallas, but it felt like a week had passed.

After he'd cleaned up at home, he'd held me for a few moments before meeting the council at his office. They'd discussed the situation until late into the night, and then Lachlan had left early this morning.

I was sure news had spread quickly through the town, but I hadn't left the house until it was time for the clan meeting. I expected a packed place, but the chairs were half-full.

Levi leaned in and whispered, "I thought the place would be bursting at the seams."

What was going on?

Lachlan sat up front. The council was in the front row

to my left. We weren't facing the crowd like him. This was his meeting to run. His actions to answer for.

A slight furrow creased Lachlan's brow as he monitored the crowd. Was he thinking the same thing? Shouldn't more people be here?

At the designated time, he rose and addressed the smattering of people. "All right. It's time to get started. What questions do you have?"

The crowd was silent.

He tilted his head. "Any questions?"

A male stood. Joseph was the son of one of the former council members. "If I may speak on behalf of the majority of Jade Hills?"

Lachlan inclined his head. Joseph couldn't request to speak on behalf of the clan, that was Lachlan's job. Speaking for the town was entirely different.

Nerves jumbled in my stomach. People would go to Joseph with their concerns. He was older than Lachlan and had always kept to himself. Was he going to challenge my mate?

"We haven't had much time to digest what happened," Joseph said. "But it doesn't matter. We've known peace since you took over. No one was brave enough to take on one, much less both, of your parents, but you did. And if the rumor's true, you did it for Venus. For us because of what it'd do to our relations with Silver clan. As far as we're concerned, well, to put it bluntly, we don't care."

Astonishment passed over Lachlan's features. "And most of the clan feels this way?"

Joseph looked around. People were nodding in the crowd. "Truth be told, we wouldn't care if you did it for no other reason. Someone had to. And since you've been in charge, I've finally been able to build up my hoard. I have treasure to pass down to my kids, and that's not something my parents were able to do."

A female, Lacey, spoke up. "I just opened the coffee shop. I grew up being told I'd better never think about making money in this town."

Murmurs traveled through the crowd.

Lachlan studied everyone for several moments. "I'll do right by the clan. Indy and I have been talking about what we can do to bring other shifters to town and create new homes for our people."

More approving nods. My stomach started to untangle. He must've talked to the council if he was willing to announce our plans. He was laying the foundation for me at the same time he was answering for his past.

I didn't realize I was smiling until his gaze landed on me. The corner of his mouth lifted, and he started fielding questions that related to business and marketing instead of what he'd done.

I glanced over my shoulder. My parents were in the back and gave me a little wave.

Today had gone well, and it was only the beginning.

Lachlan calmly chatted with members of his clan, and when the meeting was done, I walked out with Levi. People crowded around Lachlan, but I'd wait at his office.

"Since it's all cool here," Levi said, "I'm going to plan a trip to Sapphire." He veered off to the stairs.

In front of Lachlan's closed office door, Porter lingered, his gaze on the top of his shoes.

He saw me and straightened. "Indy—ma'am."

I smiled. "Indy, please. Is something wrong?" Why hadn't he been at the meeting?

"I, uh, Lachlan said I could stop by and talk to him about something."

"He's been held up at the town meeting. You could talk to him there."

"No, it's... I'd rather not have anyone overhear."

I looked around. Lachlan's office was in a quiet corner of the old armory. No one was around. "Are you in trouble?"

I thought he'd brush off my concern, but he tipped his head down. "Not me, and maybe not anymore with Dallas gone."

Hearing his name was a jolt. Last night, I had woken from a dead sleep with Lachlan's arms around me. I had dreamed of Dallas charging me, his dragon eyes focused on killing me. "Was he threatening you?"

"No?" He didn't sound sure. "Not even veiled threats. But he was interested in the property my parents bought. Like, really interested. He wouldn't quit checking on it."

"Why?"

"My parents are building, but my dad is doing the excavating himself." He sidled closer. "My dad quit working because he... he's worried he'll find bones or something."

"You think Lily is buried out there?"

"It makes sense, doesn't it? Old Man Redford was a tyrant about that land, but he didn't live out there. When he died and his son John put it up for sale, Dallas's mom tried to buy it, but my parents were friends with John."

"And then Dallas kept pestering you about it." Too much coincidental suspicion. "Tell you what, you stay here, and I'll go out to the property and take a look."

His expression turned stricken. "Do you think that's a good idea?"

"Dallas is gone," I said gently. "It should be fine. And it might give your parents some peace of mind until Lachlan can look into it more."

He'd be busy with regular town business now that the town felt comfortable going to him, but he'd want justice for Lily.

I hadn't planned much today. Every day from the meeting on had been a large blank. I'd have time to stop by the Charbonneaus' place and then check out the properties Lachlan owned and plan the next stage for after I talked to Penn. But his confidence that making a shifter-only camping resort was possible, propelled me forward. The idea would be tangible soon enough.

I drove to my parents' cabin and then hiked to the land that used to be Old Man Redford's.

A yellow excavator was parked in a clearing. I took notes. Porter's parents were doing what I hoped to do soon enough. The first stage had been to remove some trees to make room for a small house and a tiny yard. Neat logs were stacked next to the excavator.

I summoned a mental image of Lachlan's property, my parents', the Charbonneaus', and the two other landowners around the lake. I judged where the property lines were on either side.

Where was a good place to hide a body?

Closer to shore was less desirable. The lake had a natural rise and fall, depending on how wet or dry the year was. Too close to the highway that wound through the county was also a bad choice.

I'd start a hundred yards off the main road and sweep through. It'd been years since Lily disappeared. What would a grave that old look like? A mound of dirt? After two years, the underbrush would look exactly the same.

But no one had come out here to specifically look for a grave, so it was worth taking a walk through.

I wound through the trees, my progress slow thanks to the branches and the thick plants and vines. Once I reached the side that bordered one of Lachlan's properties, I started my search. This would take some time without following the trails.

A couple hours passed. I was sweaty and my muscles were gently suggesting that I wasn't used to ducking in and around trees and forcing through shoots and tangled plants. I crossed a narrow wildlife trail and several yards later, came to a stop. The plants were growing over a mound higher than those around it, making it stand out.

I tilted my head from side to side. Could it be a grave? It wasn't long and narrow, but round. I didn't know much about dead bodies, but I enjoyed watching murder shows as much as the next female. Bodies were often buried with knees to the chest. Less digging.

I went back to the thin trail and ripped at the hem of my T-shirt. It was one of my favorites, but I had no other way to mark this spot. I ripped the fabric free and tied it around a tree trunk.

Dusting my hands off, I turned. A shot blasted through the air. I jerked and looked around until a bloom of pain spread through my chest.

What the hell happened? I glanced down, realization dawning as my gaze landed on a blackened rip in the material of my shirt and the warm trickle of blood tickled my skin. A gasp sucked out of me as the pain grew and grew until I stumbled.

I'd been shot.

That didn't make sense.

A female's voice came from the distance, farther

down the trail. "It's about time you suffered. I paid those mountain lion shifters enough to find out the truth, and they almost ruined it and killed you when I couldn't watch."

I squinted, struggling to stay on my feet. Air wheezed in and out of my lungs. I wasn't a doctor, but the bullet wound was bad, too bad for me to heal on my own in the middle of nowhere.

She drew closer. A tall, gaunt woman whose face looked either haunted or as if she did the haunting. Dressed in khaki shorts and a white buttoned shirt, she looked more like she was on safari than a nature hike in northern North Dakota.

Dallas's mom. Mama Benson. She propped a rifle over her shoulder, her expression triumphant but full of hatred. "It's nothing compared to what you put my boy through."

Horror sank into my mind at the same time as my knees buckled. I pressed a hand to my wound, but the agony wasn't concentrated only there. Was there a much bigger exit wound somewhere else on my body?

My inhale was a high-pitched squeal. "You... killed..." Speaking was too much effort.

"Yes. Everyone blamed my boy when Lily was the evil one. She broke his heart." She loomed over me, keeping the gun resting on her shoulder like a soldier who had no intention of putting the enemy out of their misery. "No one hurts my boy and gets away with it."

I didn't know what crossed my face, but she nodded. She killed Lily. Had she told Dallas, or had he suspected? She had to have been uptight when the Charbonneaus bought the land.

"After I take care of you," she said, "I'll deal with that

mate of yours. He might think he's a mighty dragon, but he can't outrun a bullet, and I'll pump him so full of lead he'll be too heavy to move. Then I'll bury him alive and wait until his heart ceases to beat." Her body shook with rage. "He stole my son."

I coughed and toppled to the ground. My energy was draining, and I was succumbing to the pain.

She bent over me. "I'm going to enjoy this. I'm going to enjoy burying you next to Lily." She let out a gusty sigh. "But the Charbonneaus are suspicious. I suppose I'll have to move Lily to find a new place for all of you." Smugness crested in her eyes. "Maybe I'll plant you all where Lachlan the Coward killed his parents. A little poetic justice for them too."

LACHLAN

"She went where?" I asked.

Porter had just spilled his story, and I had to admit, it sounded plausible. Dallas might be dead, but I wanted to do right by Lily. A proper burial and answers for her family were needed.

"She said she'd take a look," he answered.

My stomach had been knotting for the last ten minutes, and I hadn't been able to figure out why. The town meeting went as well as my talks with the council last night. I couldn't wait to get home to Indy and talk about everything that happened. No more secrets hung over our future.

But my intuition screamed at me.

"I've gotta go." I sprinted out of the armory and jumped into my pickup. Peeling out of the lot, I raced to the Charbonneaus' property. The road into the place where Porter's dad had started clearing to build was rough and bumpy. My head hit the roof as I raced over them, unconcerned about the damage done to me or the vehicle.

When I got out, I was hit with Indy's scent, laced with a heavy metallic tang. She was hurt.

I opened my mouth to cry out for her, but someone had hurt her. They could be close. I took a step when a shot rang out. A grunt escaped me as an invisible force hit my shoulder.

Fuck. I ducked behind the pickup as fire ignited in my upper arm. Growling, I ripped my shirt off and struggled out of my clothing. My right arm wasn't working like it should, but I shoved the pain into the corner of my brain. One of the many unfortunate skills I learned growing up.

When I was naked, I shifted. Not many shifters could get shot and change forms, but I'd had enough practice. Another shot rang out and a metallic thud resounded around me. As soon as my wings had formed, I launched myself over my truck, my talons scraping the paint. I couldn't get the lift I needed with one of my limbs affected.

A female was emerging from the trees, her rifle raised and aimed. She fired another shot. It punctured my scales, but the bullet was slowed. I dipped and wove from the impact of my first injury but continued my charge.

Her eyes widened. Dallas's mom. Details clicked into place that I would have to examine later. I had no doubt she was responsible for Indy's injury.

Where was my mate?

She took aim again, thought better of it, and turned. She sprinted into the trees. The smell of Indy's blood got stronger.

Rage pumped me forward. I crashed through the trees. As if she determined that I wasn't letting a few spindly trees stop me, she spun and went to a knee.

She raised her rifle. I powered ahead, spitting a stream of fire. She shouted and flung herself backward. I took off her head in one chomp.

Spitting out the gore, I stopped behind her charred, dead body to shift back. My wings were tangled in branches, and the pain mingled with what was already racing through my body. I grunted through my change. Once I was swaying on two legs, I continued down the path in a lurching stop motion maneuver.

"Indy!"

Her smell clouded around me. She was in pain, and my heart ached as if she was leaving me.

I spotted her, crumpled on the path in front of me. Her eyes were closed and her energy was fading.

"Indy." I collapsed next to her, not because I was losing strength but because I didn't want to delay getting to her side. "I'm here, baby. I'm here."

I felt along her body. Her shirt was full of blood, and it didn't matter where she was injured. She was dying.

For most of my life, being born into a ruling family had been like a curse. As the oldest, I'd born much of the burden. Something I'd gladly do for my siblings. I had only wanted to justify the gifts I was born with and undo the damage my family had caused.

But now I was grateful. I was the oldest that could breathe fire and heal others. I called on the latter power now. Summoning all my energy, I funneled it into her, picturing her tissues mending tighter, her fine body closing its wounds and halting her impending death.

A small moan left her. I sagged, my own energy draining from my body when I had a similar wound. But I didn't stop until her heartbeat grew steady.

Her fingers curled around my face. "Lachlan, stop." I didn't. "Lachlan, stay with me."

Her plea got me to cease the flow of healing energy. I sank next to her, and the two of us lay on the ground, side by side like we were tossed next to each other.

"She's dead?" Indy asked.

"Yes," I managed to get out.

"Mm. Rest." Her voice was drowsy. My healing would take longer than normal, but I didn't care. She was no longer critical, and I'd make it. "Then we'll go home."

I did as my mate asked.

FOURTEEN

Indy

EDNA BEAMED AT HER NAILS. "You don't have to, you know."

"I'd miss our time together too much." I smiled.

Venus was stocking the haircut station. It'd been nice to catch up with her. And with Edna in the two weeks since Lachlan and I had recovered from our injuries.

I'd told her about my cabin rental plans and how Penn planned to set up a network where shifters would have access to an offshoot of his online teaching programs. He'd be able to verify the shifter status of those who rented. I didn't need to understand how, only that he said he could do it.

But the work would leave me with little time to take clients at the salon. After the cabins were built, rentals started, and people hired to care for the property, then Lachlan and I would be working on growing our family.

Edna's shrewd eyes gleamed. "We can grab a coffee too."

"Then who'd do your nails?" I asked.

She didn't like favors being done for her, but I spoke the truth. I'd keep doing her nails and no one else.

Venus grabbed the broom. "I'm only open two days a week. I can, but Indy is a little territorial over you."

Satisfied, Edna rose and slung her bag over her shoulder. "Next month then?"

I grinned. "Next month."

She shuffled out, and I followed. Venus offered to clean up. Penn was stopping by in an hour so they could go to Griffin's. I walked Edna to her car.

"Oh," she said before she climbed behind the wheel. "Look at that handsome mate of yours. I always knew he was one of the good ones."

Lachlan was walking down the street. He'd driven me to work. He freely admitted to being overprotective for a time until the trauma of seeing me dying in the middle of the woods faded. I didn't mind. After being attacked three times in such a short amount of time, I was a little jumpy. Time would help us each heal—together.

"I'm glad everyone else knows it now too," I said.

"They did. People like Dallas and his mom never see the good in others unless they want to exploit it." She harrumphed and slid into the driver's seat. "I'll see you at the funeral tomorrow?"

I nodded. Lily's body had been found exactly where I had marked. Her parents could finally put her to rest, and the town could mourn her loss. "I'll be there."

She stuck her key in the ignition but closed the door before I could shut it. "When you have your first kid, I'm cutting off our appointments."

I'd be sad to see that period in my life end, but time would become a precious commodity. "As long as you come over and help rock the baby so I can sleep."

Her face wrinkled with her grin. "Now, I like the sound of that deal."

She waved at Lachlan as she drove off. He wrapped his arms around me and claimed my mouth. We kissed longer than was probably decent for being in the middle of the street, but neither of us cared.

I pulled away for air. "I missed you." We'd been apart for less than two hours.

"Same. Your mom called." My parents had started reaching out directly to him. "They invited us over for supper to talk about the cabin and purchasing that property you looked at. Meatloaf."

"Mom's meatloaf is the best."

"After yours." He gave me a wink.

Mine was almost as good as Mom's, but since I made it, it was Lachlan's favorite.

We chatted all the way to my parents'. Lachlan and I were looking at more property to develop. A farm was up for sale on the edges of Jade Hills. A human with no family to carry on the business. Lachlan wanted to purchase it and hold it to sell to a dragon shifter with dreams of working the land.

We reached my parents' place. Mom swept the door open and ushered us inside. Dad met Lachlan and me with a cold beer.

"There's a half hour yet," he said. "Why don't we sit on the back porch?"

Lachlan gripped my hand, and we chose side-by-side Adirondack chairs. Dad came out of the sliding door, but Mom wasn't behind him.

I didn't think anything of it until she swept out the door. "Ta-da. I finished. You're now the proud owner of a Grandma Janet Creation." She brandished a crocheted blanket. She'd used the same color pattern Dad had chosen. Simple lines. A nice blanket, even better that Mom had made it, but when I glanced at Lachlan, I paused.

His stark expression was beyond stunned. He was poleaxed, staring. "That's a really nice blanket." He cleared his throat. "Thank you."

She adopted a wicked gleam in her gaze. "And all my kids' mates become my children, whether they like it or not."

"I never dreamed of having parents as good as you."

Mom folded the blanket and passed it to Dad. She crossed to the chair, pulled Lachlan to his feet, and wrapped her arms around him. "Call me Mom, Lachlan. You might be a Jade, but you're part of our family now."

Lachlan hugged her in return. Dad patted him on the back, then presented him with the blanket. I rose as Lachlan bunched his fists in the material.

"It's so soft," he murmured.

"I'm picky about the yarn I use." She faced Dad. "Want to help me get the table set?"

Dad read Mom's request and left.

Lachlan waited until the door was shut. "She left us alone on purpose, didn't she?"

"I think she sensed it was overwhelming for you."

"In a good way." He ran his hand over the blanket again. Those pouty lips I loved curving up. "It'll look good on top of your favorite bedspread."

He'd moved the guest room comforter into our bedroom after I'd moved back in. I told him it reminded me of sunsets at the cabin. *I always wanted to know what you thought when you looked at it*, he'd said.

I shrugged. "Mom's like that. Overwhelming in a good way, but also a little selfish. She'd dote on you—on us—but since we're the only kids left in Jade Hills, we're going to be smothered."

"I... won't mind."

"Good. Because she's working on kitty beds next." I gave him a kiss. "I love you."

"I love you. I never would've imagined being surrounded by so many good people."

"It's your reality." I wrapped my arms around him. "Our reality."

———

THANK you for reading Lachlan and Indy's reconnection. There are more dragon shifters looking for love!

When Levi Peridot goes to Cougarton to meet Briony, he's not prepared to declare himself as her mate, or to spend the rest of his time there trying to convince her he's a good idea instead of the opposite of everything she's wanted in The Dragon's Word.

ENJOY A TEASER:

THIS WASN'T GOING WELL but the cat in me couldn't tip my tail and smile pretty. I adopted a bored demeanor, hoping he was too upset to hear my heart racing. "So, about this challenge… I have a headache tonight. And I wanted to bake some bars for Gran. Tomorrow, I have some errands to run. Where am I supposed to fit you in?"

I might as well go to the hardware store across the street and buy myself a shovel because I was digging my own grave.

DJ pushed off the pickup and prowled toward me. I took a step back, terrified but willing to let him think I wouldn't fight. I would, but I'd rather make him overconfident first.

"You're not going to make it back to your little old gran, Briony. We're doing this now."

Oh shit, oh shit, oh shit. What was I going to do?

"That's not going to happen," a rich, deep voice that practically petted my nerves into submission said.

DJ jerked his head to my right. I couldn't bring myself to look. The voice wasn't familiar and I could be imagining the male coming to my rescue. Or maybe he just wanted a quiet shopping trip and would ask DJ to take the challenge elsewhere.

"Stay the hell out of this," DJ sneered, his hands curling into fists.

We weren't allowed to shift in public, but that wouldn't stop DJ from starting a fight in his human form. Cat shifters lived in the same communities their packs did, but many humans also resided in the same places.

"You dragged me into this," the delicious voice said. "As soon as you challenged my mate."

That got me to swing my head around and find out who was speaking. My gaze landed on the male from my dreams, the guy I'd been low-key obsessing over and insisting to Gran I wasn't interested in, Levi Peridot.

Wait—had he just called me his mate?

. . .

LEVI AND BRIONY'S journey to love takes a little road trip in The Dragon's Word.

———

FOR NEW RELEASE UPDATES, chapter sneak peeks, and exclusive quarterly short stories, sign up for Marie's newsletter and receive my first wolf shifter story FREE.

ABOUT THE AUTHOR

Marie Johnston writes paranormal and contemporary romance and has collected several awards in both genres. Before she was a writer, she was a microbiologist. Depending on the situation, she can be oddly unconcerned about germs or weirdly phobic. She's also a licensed medical technician and has worked as a public health microbiologist and as a lab tech in hospital and clinic labs. Marie's been a volunteer EMT, a college instructor, a security guard, a phlebotomist, a hotel clerk, and a coffee pourer in a bingo hall. All fodder for a writer!! She has four kids, an old cat, and a puppy that's bigger than half her kids.

mariejohnstonwriter.com

Follow me:

Also by Marie Johnston

More in this series

The Dragon's Oath

The Dragon's Promise

The Dragon's Vow

Jade Dragon Shifter Brothers

The Dragon's Pledge

The Dragon's Bond

Peridot Dragon Shifter Brothers

The Dragon's Word

The Dragon's Dedication

Want to try my very first shifter series?

<u>The Sigma Menace</u>

Fever Claim (Book 1)

Primal Claim (Book 2)

True Claim (Book 3)

Reclaim (Book 3.5)

Lawful Claim (Book 4)

Pure Claim (Book 5)